New TOEIC Listeni

PART 1

1. (A) (A) The men are fighting. *boxing 拳擊 = pugilism*
   (B) The men are dancing. *boxer /ˈpjuːdʒə,ˈiɜːm/*
   (C) The men are eating.
   (D) The men are reading. *n. 拳擊手四角褲*

install ① v. 安裝 ② v. 使就職

2. (A) (A) The man is installing a window.
   → *He has been installe*
   (B) The woman is writing a note. *in his new office.*
   (C) The boy is throwing a ball.
   (D) The girl is opening the door. *已就任新職*

note n. 便條, 筆記, 紙幣 v. 注意 + that / 提到 = He noted the importance

3. (D) (A) Some people are swimming in a pool. *of the problem*
   (B) Some people are at the bus stop. *in his lecture.*
   (C) Some people are watching a parade. ③ *記下 + down*
   (D) Some people are at the zoo.
   ə e
   *parade n. ① 行列, 遊行

自助餐吃 buffet

4. (A) (A) The cafeteria is not crowded. *炫耀 make a parade*
   (B) The library is closed. *of his knowledge.*
   (C) The restaurant is being remodeled. *炫耀他的知識*
   (D) The stadium is being torn down. → *These changes were*
   體育場 *paraded as progress.*
   競技場 arena

5. (C) (A) The woman is preparing some food. *v. 在...遊行*
   (B) They are in a theater. *誇耀*
   (C) They are on an airplane. *標榜*
   (D) The man is giving a presentation.

6. (A) (A) They are working on an assembly line.
   (B) They are playing in a sandbox. *組裝線*
   (C) They are helping set up a party. → *沙坑*
   (D) They are not wearing protective clothing.
   the right of assembly

assemble v. 聚集, 而裝 assembly n. 集會, 與會者, 裝配

GO ON TO THE NEXT PAGE.

PART 2

7. (C) What time is the board meeting?
(A) In the main conference room.
(B) Her name is Susanne.
(C) It starts at 1:30.

*board ① 板子 ② 伙食 We'll provide room and board for them.
n.
③董事會④舞台
→He quit the boards years ago. 好幾年前就不表演了

8. (B) Where should I put these samples for the sales presentation?
(A) Almost everyone signed up.
(B) On the table by the door.
(C) Just coffee, tea, and some pastries.

v. 登(船、車、機)
用木板封閉 + up / over
→ He boarded up the windows.

pastry 酥皮點心

9. (B) Why did you return your new laptop?
(A) It's cold this morning. 筆電
(B) Because the screen was slightly cracked.
(C) A shop in the mall.

* cracked adj. 破裂的 / 碎的 / 沙啞的
a cracked voi
(D) 瘋狂的、精神失常的
He is cracked.

10. (B) Would you care for a beverage?
(A) $500 each.
(B) A glass of sparkling water, please.
(C) I can't do it today.

喜歡(接否)/ 照料：The kids are well cared for.
討厭：She doesn't care for what she eats.
不太在乎吃這什麼

11. (A) When are you leaving for Vancouver?
(A) On Tuesday night.
(B) If I have time.
(C) Near the entrance to the theater.

動身去
入口、門口

* sparkle v.閃耀 His eyes sparkles with happiness.
① 煥發、活躍：His wit sparkles. 橾杆

12. (C) How much do you pay for your Internet service?
(A) Not very often.
(B) Sure, you can use it.
(C) $79.95 per month.

n. 火光、閃光、活力

proposal
① Proposal is easier than performance.
提議比表現容易（說比做容易）

13. (C) What should I include in my research proposal?
(A) Because I was out of town.
(B) No, we haven't found one yet.
(C) I know Dan's written a lot of them.

② She has had a proposal.
有人向她求婚

has written 丹已經寫過很多了（可以問他/可以用他的）

14. (A) Have you met Mr. Swisher, the new director of sales?
(A) Oh, we used to work together.
(B) At the board meeting next Monday.
(C) The sales department.

新的銷售主管

15. (B) Do you need any assistance <u>filling out</u> the <u>registration</u> form?
    (A) Have you been checked-in?
    (B) No, it appears to be straightforward.
    (C) These seats are empty.

*fill out ①填寫
日豐滿 =Her cheeks began to fill out.
* register v. 註冊, 申報, 正式提出

16. (B) How did you like the <u>café</u>?
    (A) No, only on special occasions.
    (B) You were right. It wasn't crowded.
    (C) Around the corner from the office.

→ People joined the march to register their opposition to the cuts in education.
參加遊行表示反對刪減教育經費
→ /kæfe/ 小餐館 /kɔ'fe/ 咖啡廳

17. (B) Was it Bob or Charlie who <u>reviewed</u> the customer surveys?
    (A) Open a customer account.
    (B) You know, I'm not really sure.
    (C) It is a 20-minute walk from here.

internet cyber | cafe 網咖
*review v. ①再檢查②評論③回顧
④檢閱
招待. 歡迎. 接待 → under review 在檢查中

18. (B) You'll be at the <u>reception</u> dinner, won't you?
    (A) In tomorrow's newspaper.
    (B) Yes, but I might be a little late.
    (C) I was <u>disappointed</u> with it.

* This disappointed his plans.
這件事打壞了他的計劃
失望

19. (C) Which room is Mr. Ball staying in at the hotel?
    (A) On Sedgwick Avenue.
    (B) I'll stay for another hour.
    (C) We can ask at the front desk.

cater to 迎合
/e/
n. 餐飲業. 承辦酒席 cater v. 提供飲食承辦 + for

20. (C) Will our <u>catering</u> staff be wearing special uniforms?
    (A) Oh, it's a bit too large.
    (B) Thanks, but we have plenty of help.
    (C) Yes, I ordered them today.

*express v. 表達, 陳述, 擠壓
→ The doctor expressed poison from her wound.

21. (C) Do you want this sent by regular mail, or do you want <u>express</u> delivery?
    (A) No, this is the wrong address.
    (B) Sign on the line here.
    (C) Regular mail, please.

n. 快車, 快遞公司
adj. 快的, 直達的, 專門的, 明確的 + order
→ They painted the house for the express purpose of selling it.

22. (A) Would you be interested in giving a <u>lecture</u> at the seminar?
    (A) When is it being held again?
    (B) I enjoyed meeting her very much.
    (C) I think you should speak with the client.

課程, 教訓 lecture on/about
Please don't lecture me.
請別跟我說教

GO ON TO THE NEXT PAGE.

23. (B) The automated sealing machine was repaired yesterday, wasn't it?
    (A) Yes, I have one of those.
    (B) No, it'll be done tomorrow.
    (C) We just received several large orders.

24. (A) Who'll be the host of the awards banquet?
    (A) Ms. Leiberman from the nominating committee.
    (B) I believe it's been postponed to next week.
    (C) You don't think we need a bigger video screen?

25. (B) Mr. Evans, I'm having problems printing the report.
    (A) I wasn't there.
    (B) You can just email it to me.
    (C) It's straight down the hall.

26. (C) The snacks and drinks are complimentary on the flight, right?
    (A) Do you prefer an aisle seat?
    (B) Run the credit card again, please.
    (C) Only in business class.

27. (C) Who's going to be the new manager of product development?
    (A) I can't wait to see your new apartment.
    (B) It's in the basement.
    (C) They're still interviewing candidates.

28. (A) Ms. Klein wants us to complete the inventory by the end of our shift.
    (A) I have a dentist's appointment at noon today.
    (B) I am looking forward it.
    (C) No, my subscription's expired.

29. (C) Weren't the windows of the building cleaned over the weekend?
    (A) Probably just read a book.
    (B) The nearby movie theater.
    (C) It rained last night.

30. (A) Does anyone have time to help me unload the delivery truck?
    (A) Larry just finished his break.
    (B) Only once or twice.
    (C) Look in the bottom drawer.

31. (A) We need to recruit experienced telemarketers to sell this product.
    (A) Maybe we should offer training.
    (B) Yes, he called earlier this morning.
    (C) It'll pass inspection, no problem.

recruit v. 招募
grow
telemarketer 電話推銷員
→ 電視、電傳、遠距離

PART 3

***Questions 32 through 34** refer to the following conversation.*

什麼東西在這區長得最好子

M : Hi, I just bought a house with some land and I'm interested in growing some vegetables.
So I need to buy some seeds. I have a question though. Could you give me some advice
about what grows best in our region?

地區、地帶、部位、領域 He is an authority in the region

W : Actually, the best way for you to get started will be one of our store's gardening classes.
There is a new beginner series starting this Wednesday night. It meets once a week for
three weeks.

of science.
新序列
園藝活動
他是科學領域等的權威

M : I'd be interested in that, but I know the basics of gardening. I just moved here so I'm
unfamiliar with such a dry climate. My needs are a bit specific.

明確的
簡單

W : Yes, on second thought, maybe the beginner's class is going to be a little too simple for you.
Here is a list of all the classes we offer at the garden center. Perhaps the intermediate
series is a better fit. If you follow me, I'll show you our selection of seeds and bulbs.

中級的
更適合的

32. (C) What is the man interested in doing?
    (A) Teaching a class.
    (B) Contacting a landscape designer.
    (C) Starting a vegetable garden.
    (D) Purchasing gardening tools.

* climate 球莖類植物
氣候、氣氛 (社會、時代的風氣、氣氛)
After the revolution, the climate of the country remained tense.
在改革之後，國家的氣氛一直很緊繃

33. (D) What does the woman suggest?
    (A) Using a Web site.
    (B) Visiting a different store.
    (C) Purchasing a book.
    (D) Attending a class.

* seed (n) 種子、根源
He was cursed for sowing seeds of discord among his friends. 播種 爭吵
他因為在朋友間挑起爭端而被咒罵

34. (A) What does the woman give the man?
    (A) A list of courses.
    (B) A textbook. 教科書、課本
    (C) Free samples.
    (D) Contact information.

(v) 在…播種：The field have been seeded with corn.
She is a walking textbook. 活教材

GO ON TO THE NEXT PAGE.

或又賣掉我目標額的一半 配額

W : Thomas, I wanted to talk to you about your sales last month. I only sold half of my quota. 等会達到預期

M : I didn't meet my monthly sales goals either. Ever since Flash Mobile started offering 自後以外 unlimited data plans, fewer customers are willing to sign up with us.

W : Management should offer incentives to attract more customers like free phones when you 办到不行   願意 sign a two-year contract. 刺激,鼓勵 / incentive payment 獎金

M : I agree. We have to figure out how we can compete in this market. 想出

35. (D) Who most likely are the speakers?   *either
   (A) Manufacturing supervisors. manufacture v.   ① adj. 任一的
   (B) Automobile mechanics. hand / make 製造   You may go by either road.
   (C) Advertising executives.
   (D) Mobile phone service plan salespeople.   She had a bag in either hand.
                                                  每一的

36. (B) What problem are the speakers discussing? (n.指令 adj.指導的,管理的)   ② 代 N. I don't agree with either
   (A) Management directives have been inconsistent.   you on this issue.
   (B) A business has been losing sales. com stand   2者中任一
   (C) New products have received poor reviews. adj.
   (D) The sales department is understaffed 不一致的   ③ conj.
                                          不協調的   She is coming either today o
37. (C) What solution does the woman suggest? 前後矛盾的   tomorrow. 或者
   (A) Soliciting customer feedback.   ④ adv.(否定句中)也,而且
   (B) Advertising online. — solicit 請求;懇求
   (C) Offering incentives to customers. → She solicited aid   If you d
   (D) Hiring additional staff.   from his close friends. 尋求協助   go, I wo
                                                                  either.

                                          市場評估
M : Good afternoon, Monica. I didn't see you at the talk about market valuation this morning.
   Did you just arrive at the conference?   結果

W : Yes, my flight from Des Moines was delayed and I had a long wait in the taxi line at the
   airport. Anyway, how has the turnout been so far? I'll be presenting later this afternoon
   and want to make sure I have enough copies of my handout. 傳單,印刷品,講義,施捨物
                              The lady never asked for a handout. 不求施捨
M : Attendance was moderate. I'd say about 150 people were there. Many of my associates
   won't be coming until tomorrow, when the heavy-hitters make their presentations. And from
   my experience, the afternoon sessions tend to be less crowded. 要事人物

W : Thanks. That's good to know. I definitely don't need more handouts, so I can save the time
   and effort. See you later.   嚴厲   → adj. 中等的,適度的
*attendance   → She is in attendance on the sick child.   → He holds moderate opinion.
到場.出席(人數),護理.   → moderate ability 能力平

52

38. (A) Why was the woman late?
    (A) She had to wait for transportation.
    (B) She was helping a colleague.
    (C) She lost her conference badge.
    (D) She went to the wrong location.

39. (D) What does the woman ask about?
    (A) Some equipment rentals.
    (B) A registration procedure.
    (C) Some changes to a schedule.
    (D) The number of attendees.

40. (D) What does the man say?
    (A) The woman may need more fliers.
    (B) The woman may have missed her session.
    (C) Fewer people attend morning sessions.
    (D) More people will attend tomorrow.

Questions 41 through 43 refer to the following conversation.

M : Hi, I ordered a ceramic tea set from your Web site, but when it arrived, some of the cups were broken. The delivery service must have dropped the package. It was clearly marked "fragile."

W : Oh, I'm sorry to hear that. However, it happens from time to time. Since your purchase was guaranteed, I can send you another set.

M : Well, I'd like to have it replaced as soon as possible, since I was planning to give it to someone as a gift next weekend.

W : All right, let me check our inventory on the computer to see if we have that exact tea set in stock.

41. (D) Why is the man calling?
    (A) A name is misspelled.
    (B) A Web site is not working.
    (C) A shipment is late.
    (D) A product is damaged.

42. (C) What does the man request?
    (A) A tracking number.
    (B) A refund.
    (C) A replacement.
    (D) A catalog.

GO ON TO THE NEXT PAGE.

43. (A) What will the woman do next?
    (A) Check an inventory. 查看庫存狀況
    (B) Call a warehouse. 倉庫、批發店、大型零售店
    (C) Talk to her manager.
    (D) Set up an appointment. 安排一個約會

* organic 有機的、不施化肥的
+ food / fertilizer 肥料
+ chemistry 有機化學
+ law 基本法

Questions 44 through 46 refer to the following conversation between three speakers.

酪梨

M : Hello, we're interested in these avocados. They're organic, aren't they?

Woman US : Yes, they are. In fact, these were grown by Dahlstrom Farms, which is just down the
    road from here. 是當地的也是有機栽種的嗎？

Woman UK : Oh, so they're local as well as organic?

Woman US : Right.
    棒棒達

M : Well, they look awesome. Give us two pounds, please.

Woman UK : That seems a bit much, dear. Aside from salads, what other uses do we have for two
    pounds of avocado? 除了

Woman US : Oh, you could make guacamole! There are free recipe cards over there that you can
    take if you'd like. /gwakə'molɪ/ 免費的食譜卡 在那裡

* aside
(adv.) ① He stood aside to let me pass
旁邊 ② Swimming is easier if you put
    feers aside.
(n) 旁白、情話、離題的話
whisper 流言耳語 / murmur

44. (B) Where is the conversation most likely taking place? use
    (A) At a restaurant. 舉行、發生
    (B) At a farmer's market.
    (C) At a flower shop.
    (D) At a tourist center.

n 用途、功能
① 用：He makes good use of his ti
    充分利用時間
② 效用、價值：What's the use of
    worrying?

45. (A) According to the American woman, what is true about the product?
    (A) It is locally grown.
    (B) It is new this season.
    (C) It is currently discounted. 最近打折了
    (D) It is only available today. 只有今天有

擔心有什麼用呢？

use up 用完 / 累
→ I have used up all the pape
→ After rowing the boat across
    the lake, he was used up.
在划船橫越整片湖之後，他累翻

46. (D) What is the British woman concerned about?
    (A) Supporting local producers. 的是什麼？
    (B) Freshness of salad ingredients.
    (C) Prices of avocados. 沙拉用料的新鮮程度
    (D) Uses for avocados.

Questions 47 through 49 refer to the following conversation.

(在田納西州)

W : I'd like to book a direct flight to Nashville on June 25th, please. Are there any flights that
    arrive in Nashville in the late afternoon?

54

M : Yes, there's a direct flight that will land in Nashville at 5:45 p.m.

W : Hmmm. That's cutting it a bit close. Is there anything earlier? I need time to set up some equipment for a 7:00 p.m. product demonstration.

M : In that case, your only option is to take a connecting flight through Indianapolis. If that's fine with you, there's a flight that will get you to Nashville earlier in the afternoon.

47. (B) What is the woman inquiring about?
    (A) Extra baggage fees.
    (B) Flight arrival times.
    (C) Payment option.
    (D) A ticket upgrade.

48. (A) What does the woman mean by "That's cutting it a bit close"?
    (A) She needs to be there earlier.
    (B) She wants more options.
    (C) She has already bought a ticket.
    (D) She is happy with the service she received.

49. (D) What does the man recommend?
    (A) Using a credit card.
    (B) Speaking to a manager.
    (C) Purchasing some travel insurance.
    (D) Taking a different route.

Questions 50 through 52 refer to the following conversation.

M : Hey, Paulina. I didn't return your phone call yesterday because I've been busy planning Ms. Walker's farewell party. It's hard to imagine her leaving us, isn't it?

W : It is. She's been the driving force of the company for how many years now?

M : Fifteen years as CEO. But listen, it's a surprise party, so don't spill the beans. Everyone will need to be in the main conference room before 5 o'clock on Friday to surprise her.

W : Um, that's a problem for me. I won't be there right at five. I have an appointment on the other side of town at four. But I will be sure to come as soon as I'm done.

50. (A) What is the main topic of the conversation?
    (A) An executive's retirement.
    (B) A budget review.
    (C) A conference presentation.
    (D) A company relocation.

GO ON TO THE NEXT PAGE.

55

51. (B) What does the man mean by "don't spill the beans"?
   (A) Arrive early at an event.
   (B) Keep some information secret.
   (C) Check an account. 帳戶 / 說明：He gave us a detailed account of his
   (D) Reserve a room. 客戶 / 理由：He got angry on this account.

   由於這個緣固他生氣了

52. (B) What will the woman be doing at four o'clock on the day of the event?
   (A) Interviewing for a new job.
   (B) Meeting a client.
   (C) Completing a report.
   (D) Attending a party.

   equip for/with ⑩ 裝備，配備
   →Our lab is well equipped.

Questions 53 through 55 *refer to the following conversation.*
   我們實驗室設備齊全
   回使有能力：Your training will equip you for your future job

W : Hi, Dennis. It's Sue Taylor. I'm afraid I have some bad news. I'm calling to let you know
that I've just missed my flight back to New York. So unfortunately, I'll have to spend another
night here in Kansas City, which means I won't make it into the office tomorrow.

M : That's not good. The V.P. of sales is coming tomorrow morning and I was counting on you
being here for this important meeting. Are you equipped for videoconferencing?
                                                        with

W : Well, there is a business center here in the hotel. But I'm not sure if it's equipped for
videoconferencing. Let me go down there and see if the center has the necessary 必需的，必要
equipment.   讓我下去看看他們   radio 無線電   videotape 錄影帶
   有沒有需要的器材   收音機   game
                                        camera
53. (D) What problem does the woman inform the man about?   cassette 卡式錄音帶
   (A) She lost her computer.
   (B) Her luggage did not arrive.   * consult
   (C) Her password is incorrect.   n.商量、請教、看病 consult the
   (D) She missed a flight. 錯過飛機   doctor
                                            查閱＝consult his notebook
54. (A) What does the man suggest? 視訊會議   during his speech.
   (A) Joining a meeting by videoconference.
   (B) Returning to a hotel.   ⑩   當顧問：The retired executive
   (C) Consulting a travel agency.   consults for several large companie
   (D) Using a car service to visit a client.
                                            consultant n.顧問
55. (C) What does the woman plan to do next?   consultation n.咨詢、諮詢
   (A) Report a complaint. 申訴抱怨
   (B) Go to a repair shop.   consultancy n.咨詢公司、顧問公
   (C) Check for some equipment. 檢查設備
   (D) Call an airline. 打給航空公司

pick sb.'s brain 問某人問題以獲取有用的信息　關於市扇銷售下滑的事　線上客戶評論

M : Carol, let me pick your brain about the declining sales of our ceiling fans. The new sales report just came out and there's a dramatic decrease in the number of ceiling fans we sold.

W : Well, I have my suspicions, but... I think it could be related to the online customer reviews. A lot of people are complaining that do-it-yourself installation is very time-consuming and difficult despite the detailed instructions.

組裝　消耗時間

打賭　即使有詳盡的指導方針、組裝起來還是很難

M : I bet you're right. What do you think about offering some kind of discount on installation? We have the manpower; it's just a matter of forming some kind of cohesive policy.

人力　形成　黏的

W : That's a great idea. I'll set up a meeting and we'll figure out how to do that.

時間安排、節目安排　有黏勁的、團結的、結合的

56. (C) What is the man concerned about?
　　(A) A scheduling conflict.
　　(B) A missing part.　n 問某、誤失
　　(C) Poor sales figures.
　　(D) Repairing furniture.

(安裝人力和公司政策要有結合)
(如:買擡匯了送安裝 or 加錢安裝等...)

adj. 令人困惑的　confuse v. 使混亂
→ You confused Tom with Tim.
你把 Tim 搞成 Tom.

57. (A) What complaint do customers have?
　　(A) A product is difficult to install.
　　(B) A Web site is confusing. *selection
　　(C) Deliveries are late.
　　(D) Selection is limited.

選擇、選果、精選品
被挑選來的人/物　she is my selection.

58. (D) What does the man suggest doing?
　　(A) Designing a survey.
　　(B) Sending an e-mail.
　　(C) Canceling an order.
　　(D) Offering a discount.

*ascend v. 上升　ascent n. 上升、登高
scal　ascensive adj. 上升的、往高的
scan　ascendant adj. 上升的、優勢的
climb　ascendancy n. 主權、優越

They made a successful ascent of the mountain. 成功登山

(up)

M : Hi, Ms. Sanchez, this is Steve Rossi from Ascendant Travel Agency. I'm calling to confirm that we'll meet as scheduled for our business lunch on Tuesday at your hotel chain's headquarters. 如同之前預訂的 (規劃好的)

W : Of course, Steve. I'm looking forward to discussing the partnership between your travel agency and the hotel chain. There's a restaurant in the west annex of the hotel lobby called Christo's at the Plaza. I thought we could have lunch there. Okay? 後面補充

M : That sounds great. By the way, where should I park? n. 隨從、隨員、出席者、侍者　adj. 隨侍的

W : You can use our parking garage next to the hotel. Bring the ticket to the front desk, and a receptionist will give you a parking pass. Just give it to the attendant on your way out.

櫃枱接待人員

GO ON TO THE NEXT PAGE.

59. (B) Why did the man call Ms. Sanchez?
    (A) To book a hotel room. 確認一個約會
    (B) To confirm an appointment.
    (C) To reschedule a meeting. 重新安排
    (D) To make a dining reservation.

annex v. ① 附加, 增添 +to
→ All insurance policy was annexed to the contract.
② 強奪, 合併: The city annexed the are across the river.

60. (B) What is located in the west annex of the hotel?
    (A) A bank. ① 健康
    (B) A restaurant. ② 適合/當
    (C) A fitness center.
    (D) A concierge. 門房

③ 得到: She annexed the first prize in the speech contest.

No one questions her fitness for the job.

annex n. 附加物
(附屬建築物)

61. (A) According to the woman, what can the man pick up at the front desk?
    (A) A parking pass.   a brochure on vacations abroad.
    (B) A discount coupon.
    (C) Travel brochure. = pamphlet   leaflet 傳單
    (D) A registration form. = boolet   = flyer

ally n. 同盟國/者
ally v. 使結盟

Questions 62 through 64 refer to the following conversation and graphic.

→ The small country allied itself to win the stronger power.

M : Hello, Ms. Oliver. My name is Phil Bates and I'm calling from Allied Industries. We've 區域銷售經理 reviewed your job application and we'd like to interview you for the position of regional sales manager. Are you available on Friday at 2:00 p.m.? → They allied against their teacher.

W : Yes, I'm available on Friday afternoon. By the way, I have a question. I remember reading 信差答覆(候選人) on the application form that candidates selected for an interview must provide at least three character references. Would you like those names now? ; provided by someone who knows you outside of work.

個性 參考 = personal reference = a recommendation

M : No, that's not necessary. We'll be sending you a follow-up email with details about the interview process shortly. I look forward to seeing you on Friday. 寄給你一封跟追是的 email

adj. 必須的, 不可缺的

62. (B) Why is the man calling?
    (A) To remind a customer. 提醒
    (B) To schedule an interview. 安排一場面試/面談
    (C) To request some sales. 要求
    (D) To respond to a message. 回覆

詢問

63. (B) What does the woman inquire about? inquire into 調查
    (A) The cost of an item.   inquire for 求見
    (B) An application requirement.
    (C) An insurance policy. → 申請要求
    (D) The name of a company.

64. (C) Look at the graphic. When should Jenna Oliver arrive at Allied Industries office?

(A) 2:10.

(B) 1:15.

(C) 1:50.

(D) 2:00.

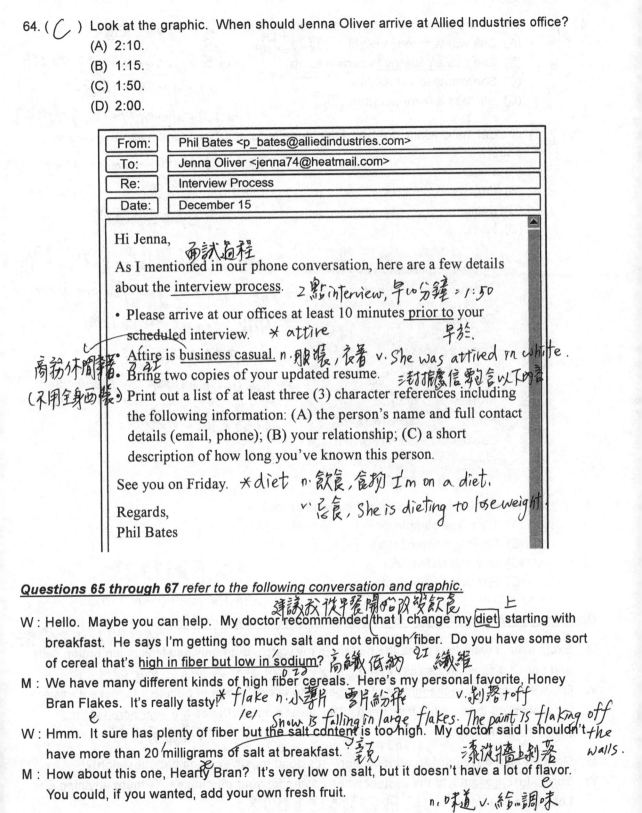

From:	Phil Bates <p_bates@alliedindustries.com>
To:	Jenna Oliver <jenna74@heatmail.com>
Re:	Interview Process
Date:	December 15

Hi Jenna,

面試過程

As I mentioned in our phone conversation, here are a few details about the interview process. 2點interview, 早10分鐘=1:50

- Please arrive at our offices at least 10 minutes prior to your scheduled interview. * attire   早於.
- Attire is business casual. n. 服裝, 衣著 v. She was attired in white.
- Bring two copies of your updated resume. 三封推薦信要含以下內容
- Print out a list of at least three (3) character references including the following information: (A) the person's name and full contact details (email, phone); (B) your relationship; (C) a short description of how long you've known this person.

See you on Friday. * diet n. 飲食, 食物 I'm on a diet.
v. 忌食, She is dieting to lose weight.

Regards,

Phil Bates

商務休閒裝
(不用全身西裝)

Questions 65 through 67 *refer to the following conversation and graphic.*

建議我從早餐開始改變飲食

W : Hello. Maybe you can help. My doctor recommended that I change my diet starting with breakfast. He says I'm getting too much salt and not enough fiber. Do you have some sort of cereal that's high in fiber but low in sodium? 高纖低納 紅 纖維

M : We have many different kinds of high fiber cereals. Here's my personal favorite, Honey Bran Flakes. It's really tasty! * flake n. 小薄片 薄片紛飛 v. 剝落 +off
Snow is falling in large flakes. The paint is flaking off the walls.

W : Hmm. It sure has plenty of fiber but the salt content is too high. My doctor said I shouldn't have more than 20 milligrams of salt at breakfast.

M : How about this one, Hearty Bran? It's very low on salt, but it doesn't have a lot of flavor. You could, if you wanted, add your own fresh fruit. n. 味道 v. 給...調味

GO ON TO THE NEXT PAGE.

65. (C) Why is the woman looking for a certain product?
(A) She wants to lose weight. 特定的商品
(B) She has an allergy to certain foods.
(C) She wants to eat healthy.
(D) She has a favorite brand. 品牌

allergy n. 過敏
→ to have an allergy to sth.
allergic adj. 過敏的
→ to be allergic to sth 對某物過敏

66. (C) Look at the graphic. Which of the ingredients does the woman express concern about?
(A) Sugar.
(B) Fat.
(C) Sodium.
(D) Fiber.

→ to have from an allergic
suffer reaction
產生/有過敏反應

Nutritional Information

Serving size: 250 grams

Calories 178

Amount per serving

Fat	7 grams
Protein	12 grams
Fiber	55 grams
Sodium	65 milligrams
Sugar	33 grams

* good for 能被信任, 能做, 有效
→ The license is good for one year.
→ Milk is good for children.
牛奶對小孩好
→ Are you good for a five-minute walk?
你有空走個 5分鐘嗎?

67. (C) What does the man suggest the woman do?
(A) Try a free sample.
(B) Go to a different store.
(C) Buy a different item.
(D) Speak with her doctor.

在做(處理)某事當中
in the middle of sth.

Questions 68 through 70 refer to the following conversation and coupon.

鋰 誰了 鈕扣型電池

M : Excuse me, I want to replace the battery in my watch, but I only see lithium ion button cells and I need a silver oxide cell. 氧化銀電池 正在重新整理所有的電池項目

W : Oh, we're actually in the middle of reorganizing our selection of batteries to make it easier for customers to find what they need. The silver oxide batteries are over here for the moment. Follow me. 暫是放在這裡

M : Great. I also have this discount coupon. It's good for silver oxide batteries, right? n.折扣 up

W : Sure. Just present it to the cashier when paying for your purchases. Is there anything else I can help you find? 拿給櫃台結帳人員看就可以了

M : No, thanks.

60

68. (A) What problem does the man mention?
   (A) He can't find an item. 找不到一項商品
   (B) He wants to return an item.
   (C) A product is defective. 有缺陷的
   (D) A coupon has expired. 到期的

目前正發生的事
69. (B) What does the woman say is currently happening?
   (A) New employees are being trained. 正接受訓練
   (B) Merchandise is being relocated. 被放到新的位置
   (C) Watch batteries are being discontinued.
   (D) A major sale is being held.
   大拍賣   正在舉行

70. (D) Look at the graphic. What discount will the man most likely receive?
   (A) Buy one get one free.
   (B) 50%.
   (C) $3.
   (D) $5.

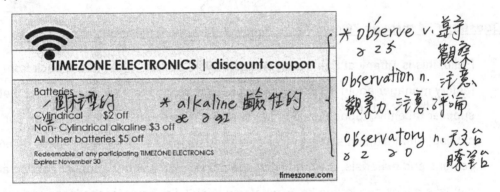

* observe v. 導守
  ϑ 25   觀察
observation n. 注意
觀察力、注意、評論
observatory n. 天文台
  ϑ 2 ϑ 瞭望台

TIMEZONE ELECTRONICS | discount coupon
Batteries 圓柱形的   * alkaline 鹼性的
Cylindrical $2 off ϑ ϑ 32
Non- Cylindrical alkaline $3 off
All other batteries $5 off
Redeemable at any participating TIMEZONE ELECTRONICS
Expires: November 30
timezone.com

PART 4

Questions 71 through 73 refer to the following telephone message.

(n)鄉紳. 大地主. 護衛 (v.) The servant squired the lady to the door.
This message is for Mr. Reynold Squire. This is Ava Nicks calling from the Oakland
你要經要求的
Hills Library to let you know that the book you've requested, *The Head on the Door*,
可以被出借了   保留2天
has been returned and is now available. We'll hold it for you for two days, but feel free
撥西至你一下
to call if you need a little extra time. The number is 667-4455. And as a reminder, the
observe (v)
library is now observing winter hours, so we close an hour earlier each day at 8:30 p.m.
Thanks Mr. Squire, and have a nice day.

GO ON TO THE NEXT PAGE.

71. (D) Why does the speaker call the listener?
(A) To ask him to return some merchandise. 商品
(B) To invite him to a writing seminar. 參加寫作研討會
(C) To offer him a membership card.
(D) To notify him that a book is available. 通知他書可以借了
通知

72. (B) What can the listener request? ＊certificate n. 證明, 證照 執照
(A) A private tour. 私人導覽
(B) Additional time. 多的時間 certification n. 認證, 保證
(C) A certificate of completion. 完成的證明
(D) E-mail notifications. 通知

73. (C) What does the speaker remind the listener about?
strain
restrict v. 限制, 約束
(A) A charity event. 慈善活動 → 提醒
(B) Parking restrictions. 停車限制 → restriction n. 約束, 限制, 限定 restrictive adj. 拘束的
(C) Reduced operating hours. 減少營業時間 operate v. 操作, 經營, 管理
(D) An application requirement. → 申請要求

Questions 74 through 76 *refer to the following telephone message.*

聽工廠經理說

Hello, this is Tiffany at Sun Valley Custom Cycle Center. I just heard back from our factory manager about the bicycle you ordered from us last week. It seems that our supplier recently stopped making the seat you'd selected. I looked through our catalog, and I did find some similar seats you might like. They are slightly different designs and materials, though. How about if I e-mail you our supplier catalog and you can take a look and let me know what you think? I'm sorry for the inconvenience.

n. 材料, 用具 → writing material 寫作用具

74. (D) Where does the speaker most likely work?
(A) At a furniture store. adj. 物質的, 肉體的, 重要的
家俱店 (B) At a real estate company. ＊exponent n. 解說者 adj. 說明的
建設公司 (C) At a construction company. output
客製腳踏車店 (D) At a custom bicycle shop. compound v. 調和, 調解, 增加 adj. 合成的, 複合的 n. 混合物

75. (D) What problem does the speaker report?
(A) An account was mistakenly closed.
(B) A factory has stopped production. 公司停止生產(運作) expound
(C) A shipment is delayed.
(D) A component is unavailable. 不可取得, 不可獲得 v. 解釋, 詳細說明
n. 成分, 材料

62

76. (C) What does the speaker offer to do?
    (A) Refund a purchase.
    (B) Meet with a customer.
    (C) Send some information
    (D) Negotiate with a supplier.

Questions 77 through 79 refer to the following instructions.

Hey guys, as you know, we've experienced an increasing number of requests for
separate checks, even though guests may be dining together. So, before we start
tonight's dinner shift, I'd like to show you how to use our new computer system to print
guest's bills separately. First, log into the point-of-sale terminal as you normally would
by swiping your key card. Then, select the split bills button, which now appears at the
left of the screen. This feature will allow you to divide the meals from your tables onto
separate bills. There shouldn't be any difficulties, but if there are, Walter's here today.

77. (A) Where most likely are the listeners?
    (A) At a restaurant.
    (B) At a supermarket.
    (C) At a clothing boutique.
    (D) At a train station.

78. (D) What are the speaker's instructions mainly about?
    (A) Some staffing assignments.
    (B) Some misplaced equipment.
    (C) A revised corporate policy.
    (D) A computer program feature.

79. (D) What does the speaker imply when he says, "Walter's here today"?
    (A) Business is slower than usual.
    (B) Staff will be observed by a supervisor.
    (C) Walter made a scheduling mistake.
    (D) Walter can assist with a problem.

Questions 80 through 82 refer to the following excerpt from a meeting.

Before we close today's meeting, I'd like to mention the free wireless Internet service
that we are now offering aboard all Orion West Airlines flights. Our competitors offer
Wi-Fi, but charge passengers to use it. It is our hope that allowing free Internet access

GO ON TO THE NEXT PAGE.

will ultimately translate to more passengers. Now, I'd like you all to take a few minutes to review a report on the projected budget for the upcoming year and provide your views on whether this proposal is feasible.

80. (A) What is being discussed?
    (A) Internet availability.
    (B) Staff retention.
    (C) Luggage restrictions.
    (D) Food quality.

81. (D) What is Orion West Airlines hoping to do?
    (A) Add international destinations.
    (B) Upgrade a computer system.
    (C) Join a partnership.
    (D) Increase ticket sales.

82. (A) What are the listeners asked to review?
    (A) A budget report.
    (B) A contract.
    (C) A marketing video.
    (D) A newspaper article.

Questions 83 through 85 refer to the following news report.

And now in local events, The Capitol Hill Annual Food Festival is next Saturday and Sunday at restaurants and public venues throughout Lincoln Park and Lower Downtown. The festival attracts hundreds of thousands of visitors every year. You won't want to miss anything, so be sure to check the Web site for a full schedule. One of the most anticipated events of the weekend will be at the Beacon Street Café, where celebrity chef, Jamie Tolliver will do a cooking demonstration and serve a special menu from 4 to 8 p.m.. on Saturday. Plan ahead, as this event is expected to be one of the most popular of the weekend and Beacon Street Café does not take reservations.

83. (D) What information should the listeners look for on a Web site?
    (A) A traffic update.
    (B) A weather forecast.
    (C) Admission fees.
    (D) An event schedule.

84. (A) Why is the event at Beacon Street Café expected to be popular?

(A) A famous chef will be preparing meals.

(B) The tourism board heavily advertised it.

(C) A musician will give a concert.

(D) The restaurant has a good reputation.

85. (B) Why does the speaker say, "Beacon Street Café does not take reservations"?

(A) To clarify a policy change.

(B) To suggest arriving early.

(C) To criticize a business.

(D) To propose a different location.

Questions 86 through 88 refer to the following telephone message.

Hi, this is Cole Nordström, and I'm the manager at Grayson Manufacturing. Last week, I ordered several parts for a broken water pump and paid an additional fee for express service, but have not yet received the parts. Meanwhile, your Web site tracking system shows that the delivery was made to our factory yesterday, but this is clearly a mistake.

Please call me as soon as possible with any information you have about my order. My telephone number is 248-0800. We need the conveyor belt to be working properly so that Fuzuki can meet our customer's deadlines.

86. (D) What is the purpose of the message?

(A) To submit an additional order.

(B) To ask for directions to a factory.

(C) To request an estimate.

(D) To complain about a delivery.

87. (C) Why does the speaker mention a Web site?

(A) It is difficult to navigate.

(B) It needs a page for feedback.

(C) It has incorrect information.

(D) It is currently inaccessible.

88. (B) What does the speaker request?

(A) A copy of an invoice.

(B) A return telephone call.

(C) Another machine part.

(D) A replacement manual.

GO ON TO THE NEXT PAGE.

Questions 89 through 91 refer to the following excerpt from a meeting.

Obviously, the firm is very proud of our team for securing the Spearhead Electronics account. This means we'll be developing the advertising campaign for the client's new line of products. Now, before the hard work begins, the senior managers would like to celebrate by taking the team to dinner. I've come up with three possible dates for the event, and I'd like your feedback. I'll follow up with an e-mail later with the details. Please let me know by the end of the day which date you prefer.

89. (C) What kind of business do the listeners most likely work for?
　　(A) An accounting firm.
　　(B) A law office.
　　(C) An advertising company.
　　(D) A travel agency.

90. (B) What news does the speaker share with the listeners?
　　(A) A ground-breaking ceremony will be held.
　　(B) A celebration is being planned.
　　(C) An important client will be visiting.
　　(D) The department is looking to expand.

91. (C) What does the speaker ask the listeners to submit by the end of the day?
　　(A) Color schemes for a waiting room.
　　(B) Requests for vacation leave.
　　(C) Time preferences for a dinner.
　　(D) Items to include on a budget.

Questions 92 through 94 refer to the following broadcast.

This is Chad Lorimer with Action 12 News, and tonight I'm reporting on an improvement to our city's transportation system that should interest many of our listeners. Commuters have long complained about bus schedules being too complicated and often changing. In response, the Municipal Transportation Department has created a smartphone app you can download to track all public buses. The app will tell you exactly where your bus is located and the approximate time it will reach your stop. No more waiting for a bus, wondering when it will arrive. I'm going to download it today.

92. (D) What is the main topic of the broadcast?
　　(A) A local election.
　　(B) A city government building.
　　(C) Online advertising.
　　(D) Public transportation.

66

93. (C) What will the listeners now be able to do?
    (A) Pay a reduced fee.
    (B) Review a document.
    (C) Track some vehicles.
    (D) File a complaint electronically.

94. (A) Why does the speaker say, "I'm going to download it today"?
    (A) To recommend a service.
    (B) To emphasize a deadline.
    (C) To take responsibility for a task.
    (D) To explain a process.

Questions 95 through 97 refer to the following announcement and sign.

Welcome to the 8th Annual Barnum Trails Hike-A-Thon. I'd like to thank KBA Sporting Goods for providing these sun visors which will come in handy at some point in the day. Before starting your hikes, I have a couple of important announcements. As you know, we usually have four hiking trail routes of different lengths. This year, unfortunately, we only have three. The 10-kilometer route is not available today because of emergency bridge work. We apologize for the inconvenience. And lastly, for everyone's safety, let me remind you to always stay on the trails which are marked with bright orange signs along the route.

95. (C) What is KBA Sporting Goods providing?
    (A) Prizes.
    (B) Refreshments.
    (C) Sports equipment.
    (D) Entertainment.

96. (C) Look at the graphic. Which route is closed?
    (A) Barnum Edge.
    (B) Barnum Delta.
    (C) Barnum Trek.
    (D) Barnum Ultra.

Barnum Trails Hike-A-Thon	
Barnum Edge	5 kilometers
Barnum Delta	7.5 kilometers
Barnum Trek	10 kilometers
Barnum Ultra	15 kilometers

GO ON TO THE NEXT PAGE.

97. (A) What are the participants reminded to do?
    (A) Follow designated trail paths.
    (B) Make a donation to an organization.
    (C) Register for an upcoming event.
    (D) Follow the directions of the officials.

Questions 98 through 100 refer to the following excerpt from a meeting and pie chart.

I appreciate your attendance at today's staff meeting. As you've read in the latest company-wide memo, we have exceeded our forecasted number of sales of our new solar water heater. This high demand is very positive, but it's pushing our production capabilities to their extreme limits. Our factory simply can't meet the new level of demand. To address our shortcomings, we have made an offer to buy one of the smaller, local manufacturers. This company currently holds 40 percent of the northeast region market share. I'm confident that we'll dominate the market in the coming years.

98. (A) According to the speaker, what was mentioned in the company newsletter?
    (A) Product sales are higher than expected.
    (B) Some executives have retired.
    (C) The company will open offices abroad.
    (D) The company was bought by a larger firm.

99. (D) What problem does the speaker mention?
    (A) Competition has become more intense.
    (B) Customers are dissatisfied.
    (C) Energy costs have increased.
    (D) The production capacity is limited.

100. (C) Look at the graphic. Which company may be acquired?
    (A) Reward Auto.
    (B) Innoba.
    (C) Coleman Motors.
    (D) Stepco Industries.

Market Share in the southeast region

Innoba 10%
Stepco Industries [PERCENTAGE] 30%
Reward Auto 20%
Coleman Motors [PERCENTAGE] 40%

READING TEST

In the Reading test, you will read a variety of texts and answer several different types of reading comprehension questions. The entire Reading test will last 75 minutes. There are three parts, and directions are given for each part. You are encouraged to answer as many questions as possible within the time allowed.

You must mark your answers on the separate answer sheet. Do not write your answers in your test book.

*regard ⓝ 問候 .best regards
事情 She was lucky in that regard.
注意.尊敬

PART 5

Directions: A word or phrase is missing in each of the sentences below. Four answer choices are given below each sentence. Select the best answer to complete the sentence. Then mark the letter (A), (B), (C), or (D) on your answer sheet. ⓥ尊重: She regards her teacher highly.

團體的.公司的.共同的 → corporate effort
有關: This doesn't regard me at all.
注重: You seldom regard my advice.

01. Corporate policy states that laptops, tablets, and other company ------- are not for private use.
- (A) property 財產
- (B) substance
- (C) rules
- (D) quality

→ The substance of his speech is that ~

v. 渡河 We ferried the river.
n. 渡輪

02. The taxi fare to the ferry terminal was ------- than expected because the driver knew a shortcut. n. 捷徑
- (A) now that adj. 提供捷徑的
- (B) less of
- (C) little more
- (D) slightly less

interdict
n. 禁止. 限制

malediction
又の

n. 詛咒. 誹謗

03. Review ------- terms of the contract carefully before signing on the final page.
- (A) whole
- (B) complete
- (C) all
- (D) each

evaluate 評估

04. ------- evaluating several delivery options, Mr. Perkins decided to send the package by local courier. 送急件的信差.快遞公司/員
- (A) After
- (B) Until
- (C) If
- (D) Beside

omit v.省略 omission n.刪除
remit v.匯款 remission n.赦免
赦免   減輕
transmit v.傳送 transmission n.送導 轉車

105. Mr. Coburn's travel schedule is always booked solid, ------- of the season. regardless
- (A) regarding 禮.不顧 in spite of
- (B) regard   irrespective of
- (C) regardless adj. 不理會的
- (D) regarded adv. 不顧一切地 He protested, but they carried on regardless.

106. Travelers should plan for longer delays than usual tomorrow because heavy rain -------.
- (A) is predicted
- (B) was predicting dictionary 字典
- (C) predicts   dictate v.n. 命令. 指定
- (D) prediction   dictation n. 命令
                     dictator n. 獨裁者

*predict 預測
say

107. The event organizer chose trophies for the athletes that were made of alloy 合金 metals because ------- gold is too soft.
- (A) pure   純金
- (B) single *trophy 戰利品. 獎杯
- (C) rich
- (D) quiet   trophy wife 花瓶嬌妻
             socialite 社交名流

108. Leslie O'Brien has submitted her ------- after nearly 25 years of reporting for *The Tulsa Chronicle*. 編年史. 紀事. 敘述
- (A) resigned
- (B) resignation *submit 繳交. 遞
- (C) resign   send
- (D) resigning

emit v.放出 emission n.
吐露   發射

109. Corvalis Allied Bank customers can easily transfer funds from one account to -------

C — 都可以當代N

adj. 結盟的, 聯姻的

- (A) one
- (B) it — adj. 又-.再- That's another matter.
- (C) another — 代名詞: 又一個.再一個
- (D) either — 任何一個 (2者之中)

110. ------- a few members did not renew their subscriptions for this year, the past quarter has been very successful.

A

- (A) Even though 即使 ＊contrary
- (B) On the contrary 不是..而是 adj. 相反的, 對立的
- (C) Despite 個
- (D) Moreover 此外 恰相反 n. 相反的事物

adv. 相反地 → Contrary to expectation, he didn't win the contest.

111. Ms. Stevenson has promised ------- all questions about the new vacation policy in a company-wide e-mail. 放假政策

B

- (A) will answer 公司都看得到的 e-mail
- (B) to answer ＊The programme is presented ←
- (C) answering by courtesy of a book company.
- (D) answer 書商提供的 、家..的好意

112. Creative Aim Consulting requires its employees to respond to e-mails as ------- as possible. 回覆信件

D

- (A) quicken
- (B) quickest
- (C) quicker
- (D) quickly

祝可要出現在銷售會議中的人.已被列在活動網頁上

113. ------- scheduled to appear at tomorrow's sales conference have been listed on the event's Web site.

B

- (A) Rooms (being)
- (B) Presenters who are scheduled
- (C) Notes → n. 目標. 對象 His proposal became
- (D) Targets the target of criticism.

114. Before assembling the new desk, make sure the floor beneath is completely -------.

C

- (A) flatter 諂媚.奉承 ＊assemble v. 聚集.集合而成
- (B) flatten v.使平坦 assembly n. 集合.集會
- (C) flat 平的.淺薄的 resemble v.相似
- (D) flatly 斷然的 a flat refusal resemblance n. 相似
  無聊的 I feel flat.

115. Passengers are required to check in forty-five minutes ------- their scheduled departure times.

B before

- (A) within para: 保護 parachute 降落
- (B) before beside: paragraph 段
- (C) into paragon m 模範. 典範
- (D) over 至高點上的. 最重要的

beyond 超 過

116. Access to Paramount Road will be ------- to southbound traffic after the road repair project begins next month.

A

- (A) limited 下個月修路案開始之後
- (B) limiting
- (C) limit
- (D) limitable

117. At Napoli Bistro, we take customer service seriously, so please remember to treat all guests with genuine -------.

B

- (A) requirement 真的. 名副其實的. 真誠的
- (B) courtesy He thanked her with
- (C) achievement genuine affection.
- (D) conference 真心感謝
  → 達成.完成.成就.成績

118. The conference rooms on the North Campus are available only ------- afternoon functions.

A 奉此

- (A) for n. 功能. 職務(責). 大集會.
- (B) in
- (C) at v. ① The machine is not functioning well.
- (D) to 起作用 ② The sofa functions as a bed at night

119. Rhodan Bicycles can be purchased online and shipped ------- to consumers.

C

- (A) direction ＊register v.
- (B) directing registered adj. 已掛號
- (C) directly 登記過
- (D) directed

120. For $25, get a personalized message ------- on a piece of Carrington gold jewelry.

D

- (A) registered progress v. 前進. 進行. 進步
- (B) progressed
- (C) polished
- (D) engraved engrave v. 雕刻. 銘記以止

GO ON TO THE NEXT PAGE.

15

得勝者老師後才會公佈評審的身份

21. During the design contest, the judges' <u>identities</u> will be kept ------- and will be <u>revealed</u> only after a winner has been announced. reveal v. 顯示.洩露

(A) curious | veil 面紗
(B) missing
(C) careful → identity 身份
(D) secret identify 認
n引入.通風口 → identification 證出.身分證明

22. The intake filters of your Unger air conditioning unit must be routinely ------- to keep the appliance functioning properly. 2 q2 器具.設備.應用

(A) have cleaned
(B) clean
(C) cleaned
(D) of cleaning

23. <u>Mr. Garcia</u> will give the presentation to Vivacon's representatives 代表 since he has worked with them on previous campaigns. 宣傳/競選運動/戰役

(A) his v. 從事運動/競選/作戰/出征
(B) himself
(C) he ← Your invention is very practical
(D) him Practical experience 實際的

實用的

24. The mayor's press conference meeting 記者會 ended so ------- that few reporters were allowed to ask questions.

(A) <u>practically</u> 實際上.事實上,幾乎,差不多
(B) abruptly 突然地 abrupt adj. 突然的
(C) obviously
(D) broadly 寬度地.粗枝地 Her job is broadly similar to mine. 大體相似

25. The next Technology Expo will open on a date that ------- the software developer's tenth anniversary.

(A) inquires about
(B) responds to 對...作出回應(回答)
(C) coincides with 與...相一致. coincide
(D) translates to 調動.轉移 v. 一致符合

→ translate into 使轉化/翻譯/辭釋
The novel has been translated into many languages.

126. If a virus makes it into one user group, it will <u>affect</u> not only those computers ------- the entire network. affect v. 影響

(A) just as affection n. 感情.疾病
(B) but also affectation n. 假裝
(C) provided that affectionate adj. 摯愛的.親切的
(D) even if n. 賣藥室.研究室.化學藏.藥廠

127. Ferguson Laboratories has announced the development of a ------- <u>lifesaving</u> drug to treat diabetes. 救命的
lifesaver
(A) formally * provided that n. 救命者.工具
(B) originally 倘若.以~為條件
(C) carefully → I'll go, provided that you go too.
(D) potentially → provided that there is no opposition, we shall hold the meeting here.

strive 努力奮鬥

128. Many companies <u>strive</u> to be ranked among the region's best workplaces ------- attract the best job candidates.

(A) so that 努力要被評選為本區的最佳工作場所
(B) causing 以爭到最好的工作候選人
(C) towards
(D) in order to

grow 補充.徵兵.招募 努力

129. All existing <u>recruitment efforts</u> must be reviewed ------- the funding cuts announced yesterday by the budget committee. 預算會議

(A) as a result 結果.因此
(B) because of 因為
(C) in front of 在...之前
(D) across from 在...對面

著陸

130. Although Hurricane Stephan is not ------- to make <u>landfall</u> on Saturday, the Forester Company annual picnic has been <u>postponed</u> until August 3. 年度野餐

(A) likely | be likely to 有...的可能
(B) likes
(C) liking 延期
(D) likeness

Directions: Read the texts that follow. A word or phrase is missing in some of the sentences. Four answer choices are given below each of the sentences. Select the best answer to complete the text. Then mark the letter (A), (B), (C), or (D) on your answer sheet.

Questions 131-134 refer to the following notice.

Levis Laboratories 3-D Printer Policy

This 3-D printer is for the ------- use of Production Department employees.
                                131.

Workers from other departments must use the standard printers found on

the second floor. Production Department staff members may print up to 5

objects per week without a manager's authorization. Staff must receive

managerial approval to make ------- items.
                              132.

Note that 3-D printing ------- for development and business purposes only.
                        133.

No personal printing is permitted. -------.
                                    134.

Thank you for your cooperation.

---

131. (A) peculiar
     (B) unusual
     (C) customary
     (D) exclusive

132. (A) additional
     (B) required
     (C) such
     (D) these

133. (A) is intended
     (B) should intend
     (C) intends
     (D) intending

134. (A) The black-and-white printers have been upgraded to make a limited number of color copies
     (B) The second-floor printers will be replaced during the month of September
     (C) Objects created with the 3-D printer are for internal use by Levis Labs and external marketing associates
     (D) Technical Support maintains all printers and copiers

GO ON TO THE NEXT PAGE.

17

Questions 135-138 refer to the following e-mail.

From:	Gerard James <james@louisville.org.gov>
To:	Wendy Crowder <crowder@rapture.com>
Re:	Membership
Date:	October 5

Dear Ms. Crowder,

I hope you are enjoying your Louisville Museum of Natural History membership. Please note that your membership ------- on December 1. **135.** By renewing your membership now, you can take advantage of a special 25 percent discount. This offer is good only ------- October 31. Simply enter the code AUG144 **136.** at the checkout page by this date. All of us at the Louisville Museum of Natural History appreciate your past support and hope you renew soon so that you may continue to receive all the benefits of membership without -------. **137.**

And remember, our members receive two complimentary tickets to our featured exhibition, Ancient Egyptian Artifacts. -------. As a member, **138.** you can preview it at a special reception on November 27.

Sincerely,
Gerard James
Director of Membership
www.louisville.org.gov

135. (A) has expired
(B) will expire
(C) to be expiring
(D) must have expired

136. (A) inside
(B) against
(C) excluding
(D) until

137. (A) interrupting
(B) interruption
(C) interrupts
(D) interrupted

138. (A) Rather, we will announce the changes on November 15.
(B) We thank you for completing the membership survey.
(C) Our membership fees have increased this year.
(D) This exhibition opens to the public on December 3.

18

Questions 139-142 refer to the following e-mail.

From:	Maggie Green <butterfly77@hugmail.com>
To:	Customer Support <support@shazamtech.com>
Re:	Order ST-0081294
Date:	April 12

To Whom It May Concern,

I recently purchased a pair of shoes from the Wox Tech Web site. When I first received the shoes a month and a half ago, I tried them on. ------- , when I went to wear them for the first time yesterday, I
139.
noticed slight imperfections in the stitching of both toecaps. I know that any ------- items must be returned or exchanged within
140.
three days and that my purchase is no longer within the required time frame. -------.
141.
If the shoes ------- out, I would be happy to choose another pair of
142.
shoes at the same price.

Please let me know what my options are.

Sincerely,
Maggie Green

(handwritten annotations: However; 1,5個月; n.不完美、缺陷 = defect = flaw = deformity（連漆不圓不完美）; defective 縫、紉 101 鞋頭; 我知道我已經超過期限，但還是希望…; are sold 如果我買的那雙賣完了，我可以選別雙價格相同的; ＊slight (adj) ①輕微的 She has a slight fever, 小發燒 ②瘦小的 She is a slight girl. (v.)輕視: He was highly respected because he slighted no one.*)*

139. (A) Still 仍然
(B) However 然而
(C) Therefore 因此
(D) Additionally 此外
(B marked)

140. (A) accepted
(B) ill-fitting 不合身
(C) mistaken 錯誤的，被誤解的
(D) defective 有缺陷的 不完美的
(D marked)
He was mistaken about her age.

141. (A) This policy has been extended to at least 60 days 這項政策已被延長至勤60天
(B) Nevertheless, I am asking you to kindly make an exception adv.仍然，不過，然而，希望您開個例外
(C) Please add a credit to my account to be used for future purchases 拜把錢兌到我帳戶裡，以後可以用
(D) I sent the package back to you two weeks after I received it 我收到2周後就把包裹寄回去給你們了
(B marked)

142. (A) be selling
(B) having been sold
(C) are sold
(D) will sell
(C marked)

GO ON TO THE NEXT PAGE.

Questions 143-146 refer to the following e-mail.

From:	Tony Norman <tnorman@creativeaim.com>
To:	Annie Baker <abaker@fanmail.com>
Re:	Incentive program
Date:	June 5

Hi Annie,

I'm so pleased that I got to meet with you in Miami. At dinner, you mentioned the customer incentive program you ran last year. You said the program ------- a contest that monitored customer feedback, with
143.
prizes for the employees receiving the most positive responses. I was impressed with how the program improved ------- and morale. It sounds
144.
like ------- the best way to let employees know how much their contributions
145.
are valued. -------. Would you be able to talk with me about how you
146.
monitored feedback and the types of prizes you offered?

I look forward to hearing from you.

Sincerely,
Tony

---

143. (A) will involve
(B) to involve
(C) involving
(D) involved

144. (A) necessity
(B) productivity
(C) expenses
(D) preference

145. (A) as if
(B) instead of
(C) about
(D) like

146. (A) I would be happy to work on the sales presentation
(B) I canceled the meeting with our colleagues
(C) I would like to do something similar at my company
(D) I plan to hire additional representatives

Directions: In this part you will read a selection of texts, such as magazine and newspaper articles, e-mails, and instant messages. Each text or set of texts is followed by several questions. Select the best answer for each question and mark the letter (A), (B), (C), or (D) on your answer sheet.

*along ⓘ 順著 (adv) 向前. 起 He sang loudly as he walked along. 列：I'll be along
Questions 147-148 refer to the following notice. Come along with me. in a minute.
get along → 相處 We get along just fine. → 新聞 It's time for getting along.
→ 進展 How is he getting along with his studies?

NOTICE – MOCA TENANTS AND VISITORS!

住戶(所)
＝resident ＝occupant ＝dweller ＝inhabitant

The sidewalk |along| Foothills Parkway is scheduled to be

repaired next week. Due to safety concerns, the main

entrance of the Museum of Contemporary Art (MOCA) will
adj. 詩代的. 同時代的 n. 同代人. 同時期的
人物

be inaccessible from Monday, December 19 through Friday,

December 23. advise v. 勸告, 通知, 商量   act on sb's advice 按某人的勸告行事

advice n. 忠告, 消息, 報告 → I act on the lawyer's advice.

MOCA tenants and visitors <u>are advised to</u> use the south entrance

on Colorado Avenue. To get to the reception desk on the second
climb   raise light
floor, take either the escalator or the elevator, both of which can
手扶梯   電梯
be found at the south entrance of the building.

＊temporary 短暫的；臨時會發生的

＝momentary 瞬間的

→ We feared a momentary attack. 擔心臨時發生的攻擊

147. What is the purpose of the notice?

B (A) To introduce changes to certain
    security measures. 安全措施
   (B) To announce the temporary closure
       of an entryway. 入口(處)
   (C) To report the vacancy of a property.
   (D) To disclose the new location of a   空房. 位. 缺
       company. 揭露 ＝reveal ＝uncover   職

148. What is suggested about MOCA?

C (A) Many people live there.
   (B) It will reopen on Friday.
   (C) The main entrance is on Foothills
       Parkway.
   (D) The renovation project will take
       one month.

GO ON TO THE NEXT PAGE.

From:	Jamie Keltner, Project Manager
To:	Corporate Resource Team
Re:	Overseas Support
Date:	October 10

Hi Team,

At next week's strategy session, we will address the specific needs of our company representatives working at our new overseas retail locations. Our goal is to have each employee fully trained in marketing our products and in client retention. I'm requesting that each of you be ready to present two ideas on the best ways to provide them with training and logistical support at levels comparable to their domestic counterparts.

Thanks,
Jamie Keltner
Team Lead, Echoplex Instruments

149. According to the e-mail, what is true about Echoplex Instruments?

(A) It markets symphonic instruments.
(B) It has an international presence.
(C) It plans to open several more stores.
(D) It just produced a new line of products.

150. What does Mr. Keltner ask employees to do?

(A) Accept overseas deployment.
(B) Contact clients.
(C) Attend a training session.
(D) Prepare for a meeting.

Read This First - Important Information!

At Colby-Sanford Inc., our reputation is based on our high-quality, easy-to-assemble cabinets, and we guarantee total satisfaction with your purchase.

Prior to assembling your Colby-Sanford product, check the parts list to make sure that all parts have been included in the box.

If your item is missing any parts, for instance, assembly hardware, or if it has been damaged during shipping, DO NOT return the product to the retail location from which you purchased it; retailers are only vendors and do not carry replacement parts. Instead, contact us directly, and we will send you the item(s) required free of charge. You can reach us by:

- visiting us at www.Colby-Sanford.com to order replacement parts online;

- sending us an e-mail at parts@Colby-Sanford.com; or

- calling us anytime at 202-767-1111

151. What is the purpose of the information?

(A) To offer incentives to loyal Colby-Sanford vendors.

(B) To direct customers to nearby retail locations.

(C) To inform customers where to obtain product assembly.

(D) To notify customers how to resolve a problem involving their purchase.

152. What is suggested about Colby-Sanford, Inc.?

(A) It recommends returning damaged goods to the retailers.

(B) It has a new assembly hardware system.

(C) It supplies a product catalog with each order.

(D) It has customer service representatives available at all times.

GO ON TO THE NEXT PAGE.

Maria Cicero [8:01 A.M.]

我要開始為婚禮擇行做準備工作了

Hey Lance. I'm at the restaurant. I need to start doing prep work for the wedding reception this afternoon. But I don't have a key and the kitchen door is locked.

Lance Kudgel [8:03 A.M.]

主廚Poncey不在那裡嗎? 通常有大活動那天他都會早點出現(早點到)

Chef Poncey isn't there? He usually shows up early on the day of a big event.

Maria Cicero [8:05 A.M.]

(人員)

對呀, 我也很困惑 而且洗碗團隊也不在

Right? I'm confused. And the dishwashing crew isn't here, either. You'll be in this morning, won't you? 你今天早上會來 對吧

Lance Kudgel [8:07 A.M.]

我要去公司總部參加一個會議的路上

Um, no. Actually, I'm on my way to a meeting at corporate headquarters, but I'll swing by and let you in. Give me 15 minutes.

= drop by 我會順路是局去 幫你開門

Maria Cicero [8:08 A.M.]

OK. I'll wait in my car. I'm parked underground. Text me when you get here?

電視.廣播主持人 / anchor n.錨 主持

新聞主播 固定: We anchored the tent with pegs.

153. Who most likely is Mr. Kudgel?

B
(A) An anchorman.
(B) A restaurant manager.
(C) A bartender.
(D) An executive chef.

154. What does Ms. Cicero most likely mean when she writes, "I'm confused"?

D
(A) She received the wrong paperwork.
(B) She doesn't know where her key is.
(C) The band should be there already.
(D) The chef usually arrives early.

24

Visiting Portsmouth? These are must-see destinations!

Waterville Valley Resort

Enjoy hiking, backpacking and mountain bike trails that lead to backcountry areas of the surrounding White Mountain National Forest. A restaurant and swimming pool (both open in summer only) overlook the lake. Groceries, gifts and snacks can be purchased at the resort gift shop.

The River Casino and Sports Bar

On the Nashua River. A spectacular replica of the original Eiffel Tower in Paris. Open daily 10 a.m. – 10 p.m.; $15 admission includes souvenir program and elevator ride to observation deck.

George Washington House Museum

930 S. Westmoreland Blvd, ☎(479) 444-0066. The house Washington lived in while he taught at the University of New Hampshire. It has been turned into a small museum with a gift shop and a short tour. $5 adults, $1 kids.

The University of New Hampshire

The main campus, home of the Wildcats, is located at the west end of Dickson Street. "Track Capital of the World" and renowned center of NEC sports, the campus is situated atop one of the many hills in the town. Check out the many stadiums (football, baseball, track, gymnastics, basketball, soccer, etc.) and the many, varied academic buildings on campus. Also, the New Hampshire Union has a coffee shop and a movie theater, and the K.T. Mullins Library has free Internet access. Just ask the circulation desk.

155. What is purpose of the information?

(A) To highlight the accomplishments of local athletes.
(B) To give transportation information.
(C) To describe notable landmarks.
(D) To provide a schedule of event.

156. What is indicated about the K.T. Mullins Library?

(A) It is closed on Monday.
(B) It is located inside the Washington House Museum.
(C) It features sporting events.
(D) It offers free Internet access.

157. According to the information, what do the Eiffel Tower replica and the Washington House Museum have in common?

(A) Both are located in the White Mountain National Forest.
(B) Both display historical artifacts.
(C) Both offer guided tours.
(D) Both charge a small admission fee.

GO ON TO THE NEXT PAGE.

25

FIRST AMERICAN MILWAUKEE EXEC RECEIVES AWARD
BY LOU DOBBS

WAUKESHA – The Wisconsin Land Title Association (WLTA), one of the state's oldest trade associations, presented Ronald Reich, a Vice President and the State Agency Manager for First American Title Insurance Company, with the esteemed Title Person of the Year Award during the WLTA Annual Conference and Business Meeting in Waukesha, July 20. The award, which is the highest honor bestowed by WLTA, recognizes significant and long-time contributions to the title industry and the association. "Ronald has been a constant champion for our association and the title industry in Wisconsin, and we are honored to present him with this prestigious award," said Lou Souza, Executive Vice President and CEO of WLTA. "The contributions he has made as part of our association leadership are too many to name, and we are privileged to have him among our ranks."

Reich has been an active WLTA member for a number of years, serving on numerous committees as both a member and chairman. He served as WLTA president (2009-2010) and currently serves as a trustee of the WLTA Political Action Committee and co-chairs the WLTA PAC Fundraising Group. Reich works out of First American's Milwaukee office and has been with the company for 16 years. In his 29- year title insurance career, most of his time has been devoted to working with independent agents as an agency manager. He managed an agency for three years in Milwaukee. Before ne entered the title industry, Reich spent four years with Sturgeon & Wimbley, where at the age of 24, he was one of their youngest sales managers ever. Reich earned a Bachelor of Science degree in business administration from the University of Texas and enjoys spending his free time with his wife, Leah, and their four children.

158. What is most likely true about Mr. Reich?
  (A) He led efforts to simplify the title process.
  (B) He designed a new type of insurance.
  (C) He served on a WLTA committee.
  (D) He has received several awards from the WLTA.

159. What was Mr. Reich's job at Sturgeon & Wimbley?
  (A) Sales manager.
  (B) Company spokesperson.
  (C) Construction manager.
  (D) Building supervisor.

160. What happened 16 years ago?
  (A) Mr. Reich moved to Waukesha.
  (B) Mr. Reich began working at First American Title Insurance Company.
  (C) The WLTA revised its membership requirements.
  (D) The WLTA first presented its award.

Questions 161-163 refer to the following notice.

PUBLIC NOTICE

Utility Construction Scheduled for Martha Swann Park

MARCH 15 - As part of the Basement Flooding Protection Program, the City of Jacksonville will be modifying and upgrading the combined sewer system by implementing an underground storage tank in Martha Swann Park.

A diversion chamber will be constructed at the intersection of Napoleon Avenue and Spencer Avenue. These will also be sewer upgrades on Walker Boulevard between French Street and the park as part of this project. A map of the construction area can be accessed at:

http://www.cityplanning.gov/jacksonville_sewer

Construction is expected to begin Monday, April 6 and be completed in one year. Your co-operation and patience during the construction period is appreciated.

Important Advisory

Many people have landscaping, fences, irrigation systems or other physical features in front of their home which are within the City property limits. These may be in the way of the construction. In such cases, residents are advised to remove these items prior to the beginning of construction in order to avoid unnecessary damage. The City will not be responsible for damage to any privately-owned items installed on the City's property.

City of Jacksonville Department of Public Works

161. What is indicated about the construction project?
(A) It will cause flight delays.
(B) It will result in better access to the park.
(C) It will take place over a period of one year.
(D) It will include emergency repairs.

162. When will the roadwork initially begin?
(A) On a Monday.
(B) On a Friday.
(C) On a Saturday.
(D) On a Sunday.

163. What action does the City recommend?
(A) Taking public transportation.
(B) Avoiding driving during peak hours.
(C) Using the west entrance to Martha Swann Park.
(D) Removing items from City property.

GO ON TO THE NEXT PAGE

Sea Pines is Back on the Map!

SEA PINES (January 24) – According to a year-end study conducted by the Atlantic Coast Hospitality Index, tourism at our beaches improved dramatically this last summer, and the hotel industry showed greater profits this year than last. Hotel occupancy averaged 102 percent during the peak summer months. This was a big increase from last summer's average of just 77 percent. –[1]–

Last spring, Sea Pines saw the opening of the area's largest hotel, The Regal Palms Resort and Casino. The new resort was at full capacity nearly every weekend during the summer. Weekday occupancy also surpassed expectations. –[2]–

The hotel's manager, Savannah Richards said, "Tourists were thrilled with the array of amenities offered, including 24-hour dining options, a free shuttle between casinos, and great value for their money. In fact, many have already reserved rooms for next summer. –[3]–

Sea Pines has become the most popular tourist destination in the region, with about 15 percent more beachgoers than Myrtle Beach, its biggest competitor. –[4]–

Tourists continue to visit the area after the prime summer months, keeping hotel rooms occupied longer.

164. What is the purpose of the article?

(A) To discuss job opportunities in the hotel industry.

(B) To compare the economies of two neighboring cities.

(C) To announce the opening of a new hotel.

(D) To provide information about the local tourism industry.

165. What is suggested about The Regal Palms Resort and Casino?

(A) It has contributed to the rise in tourism.

(B) It has forced smaller hotels to close.

(C) It attracts a criminal element.

(D) It will expand to Myrtle Beach.

166. What is NOT indicated about Sea Pines?

(A) Its beach is more popular than Myrtle Beach.

(B) Its new hotel employs Ms. Richards.

(C) It offers good value for consumers.

(D) It recently held a beach cleanup weekend.

167. In which of the positions marked [1], [2], [3], and [4] does the following sentence best belong?

"Experts attribute this to the increasing number of casinos in the area, overall lower prices, and an abundance of new restaurants, hotels, and attractions."

(A) [1].

(B) [2].

(C) [3].

(D) [4].

Handwritten notes:

* element
n. 元素、要素、成分
   特定的一群人
in one's element
如魚得水、在行、做某人擅長的事
→ He is in his element when playing basketball.

* conduct v. 率領、負施、處理、傳等
  lead
conductor n. 領導者、指揮
conduce v. 有益、導致
conducive adj. 有助益的
→ Exercise is conducive to good health.

* expert
n. 專家 = master = adept
adj. 熟練的、有經驗的
   專家的、內行的

* attribute n. 屬性、特性
   attribute 性質、原因）歸於 + to

邻近的
捐助、幫助
下

From:	Karen Claibourne
To:	All Employees
Re:	Convention
Date:	May 4

Proposal.doc 23.0 KB

Hey guys and gals!

The 10th annual Great Midwestern Sales and Marketing Convention (GMSMC) will take place from June 9-12 here in Louisville. Convention organizers have asked local e-commerce specialists to contribute by giving a keynote speech, leading a seminar, or working in the exhibition hall. ---[1]---.

Our chief executive officer, Sanjit Darvish, wants us to take advantage of this excellent opportunity for Darvish Concepts to achieve visibility on a national stage. It is sure to help us to expand our client base. Mr. Darvish has already agreed to give a keynote speech about using survey results to create successful e-commerce marketing campaigns. ---[2]---.

I am organizing our company's booth for the exhibition hall. If you would like to help, please come to Room C556 at 2:00 P.M. next Monday, May 11, for a planning meeting. ---[3]---.

If you would like to lead a seminar, please complete the attached proposal form and return it to me by May 18. This will help me ensure that none of our seminar topics overlap. ---[4]---. Seminar ideas will be discussed and approved at a manager's meeting on May 25.

168. What is the purpose of the e-mail?

B

(A) To apologize for missing a deadline. 錯過期限而道歉

(B) To invite staff to submit an application. 邀請員工繳交申請表

(C) To request responses to a marketing survey. 要求回應一個行銷調查

(D) To remind staff to apply for travel reimbursement. 提醒員工申請
（下） 旅行補償

169. What is suggested about Darvish Concepts?

B

(A) It is hosting the GMSMC.

(B) It is located in Louisville.

(C) It has been in business for ten years.

(D) It serves clients throughout Kentucky.

170. According to the e-mail, why does Mr. Darvish want employees to participate in the GMSMC?

A

吸引新客戶
(A) So they can attract new clients.

(B) So they can listen to his keynote speech.

(C) So they can learn new marketing strategies. 行銷策略

(D) So they can share the results of the survey.

171. In which of the positions marked [1], [2], [3], and [4] does the following sentence best belong? 要和演講細節有關

D

"You may present alone or with a partner."

(A) [1].

(B) [2].

(C) [3].

(D) [4].

＊ <u>reimbursement</u> 退款
報銷. 賠償
reimburse → 報帳. 補償
≠
compensate → 貼補. 補償
（因公司某方面不足. 用其他方式
來補公司福利. 西淳. 紅利都算）
compensation package.

＊ earnings 所有的收入
wages 按小時的工資
salaries 按月/年給的

＊ job hunter 找工作的人
candidate 應徵的人
personnel 人事 + department
+ training
employee 公司的員工/
（屬於公司的人）
staff 一個部門所有的職員/部屬
He is my staff.

＊ assignment 任務. 作業
errand 以前（任務）
現在（雜務）
errand boy / run errands.

GO ON TO THE NEXT PAGE.

*vacuum   *vacuum flask 保溫瓶
bottle = thermos
①真空 ②與外界隔絕的狀態
→ She is living in a vacuum.

Matt Pecora [9:05 A.M.]
Deandra, when we last spoke, production was nearly finished on the boxes and other packaging for Rothschild's. Where are we now?

a carton of milk   盒牛奶
紙盒   cigarettes 盒香煙

Deandra Whiteside [9:06 A.M.]
① 真空袋
The vacuum-seal bags, folding cartons and take-out boxes were supposed to arrive at Rothschild's warehouse on Monday, but the hurricane really messed up our delivery schedule.
把某物弄亂/弄髒/搞砸

Matt Pecora [9:07 A.M.]   well aware of
sth.
Are they aware of this?   充分了解到, 意識到

Tina Shultzer [9:08 A.M.]
They should be, but I was waiting to hear from the drivers. Dylan, what have you got?
乙②

Dylan Kubinski [9:09 A.M.]
I spoke with them early this morning. They're back on the road now, but they're separated. They should start arriving at Rothschild's warehouse sometime in the middle of the night. Not sure in what order though.   adv. 然而 It was a hard job,
還是   he took it though.
這個困難的工作, 但他還是接了

Tina Shultzer [9:11 A.M.]
Ok. I'll tell them to have someone on-hand to accept the delivery. How many pallets are we talking again?   ① 在手頭 ② 在場
① 工   搬貨的板子. 托盤. 調色板 They have a large supply of goods on hand.

Deandra Whiteside [9:12 A.M.]   hold
24. As long as the truck containing the folding cartons gets there tonight, we should   contain v. 包含. 容納. 容居   contained adj. 克制的
be in good shape.   沒問題   containment n. 包含. 牽制. 圍堵   被控制的
→ He is in a good shape to win the contest.

Matt Pecora [9:13 A.M.]   ① 身體狀況好 ② 情況好→ 有望奪標
The contract is for us to provide packaging materials for all of Rothschild's products, not just the smaller ones. Let's make sure we get everything to them ASAP. Tina, get someone on the phone and let them know for sure what's going on.

172. What type of business do the people most likely work for? 供應餐廳需求的公司

(A) A restaurant supply company.

(B) A trucking company. 貨車運輸公司

(C) A packaging manufacturer. 包裝製造商

(D) A food delivery service. 食物運送服務

(handwritten "C" next to question)

173. What problem are the people discussing?

(A) An order was incorrect. 報告工作情況

(B) A driver did not report for work.

(C) A shipment was delayed. 運送遲了

(D) A warehouse was destroyed.

倉庫. 大型零售店

warehouseman 倉庫老闆

(handwritten "C" next to question)

174. What will Ms. Shultzer most likely do next?

(A) Call a driver.

(B) Contact the client. 聯絡客戶

(C) Cancel a shipment. 取消運送

(D) Place an order.

(handwritten "B" next to question)

175. At 9:08 A.M., what does Ms. Shultzer most likely mean when she writes, "What have you got"?

(A) She thinks Mr. Kubinski should deliver some boxes.

(B) She needs Mr. Kubinski to drive to the warehouse.

(C) She wants Mr. Kubinski to provide delivery information. 提供運送資訊

(D) She expects Mr. Kubinski to pay the drivers. 期待. 預期

認為: I expect you a righ

(handwritten "C" next to question)

(A) supply and demand 供需

Our medical supplies are running short.

醫療 補給品

supply n. 生活用品, 生活費

→My father has cut off the supplies.

＊單字補充

1. Will being around a puppy _____ your allergies?

(A) affect ✓

(B) effect

2. I just _____ Joe of the fact that his pet is no longer welcome here.

(A) appraised 評估, 估計

(B) apprised 通知 ✓

3. Can you stick around and help _____ the situation?

(A) defuse 平息 ✓

(B) diffuse 擴散

GO ON TO THE NEXT PAGE.

From:	Martin Dietrich
To:	All Foursquare Design employees
Re:	July Renovations
Date:	May 23

✉ Schedule.xls (121.7 KB)

As most of you are aware, our schedule will be somewhat disrupted during the first week of July. Various rooms and offices will need to be vacated for certain periods to allow work crews to repaint, replace old furniture, and install new carpeting. Affected employees will need to box up all their office items by 5:00 p.m. on the day before their room is scheduled for work (please see the attached schedule). Two teams of workers will be on-site, so more than one room at a time will need to be vacated. Note that any rooms due for work on Monday must be packed up and vacated by Friday afternoon, June 29.

Boxes will be provided. Leave your boxes in the rooms for the work crews to remove. Please label them with your name and office number so that the crews can return them to the correct offices once the work is complete. Please make arrangements to continue working on your assignments while the work crews are in your rooms. Conference Room C will remain available to be used as a workspace for the entire week. Another possible option is to request permission from your supervisor to telecommute for one or two days.

Please have patience with these temporary inconveniences and do not hesitate to contact me with any questions or concerns.

Martin Dietrich, Office Manager

34

FOURSQUARE Remodeling Schedule – July 2 to July 6

Date	Work Scheduled	Affected Employees
Monday, July 2	Office 1103	Al Spears Mickey Gorshak
Tuesday, July 3	Conference Room A	
Wednesday, July 4	Office 1108	Sandra Tonklin Luke Taylor
Thursday, July 5	Conference Room B	
Friday, July 6	Office 1101	Steve Chu Elliot Delaney Carmela Nastasia

176. Why was the memo sent to employees?
(A) To request feedback about new work facilities
(B) To address their complaints about building maintenance.
(C) To inform them of upcoming renovations.
(D) To announce that the firm will be relocating.

177. What are employees instructed to do?
(A) Submit expense reports.
(B) Schedule a meeting with their supervisors.
(C) Indicate which office supplies are theirs.
(D) Update their contact information online.

178. What is stated about Conference Room C?
(A) It will be renovated on July 6.
(B) It will be available for video conferencing.
(C) Employees may gather there for work.
(D) A scheduling meeting will be held there.

179. When should Ms. Tonklin be ready to vacate her office?
(A) On March 12.
(B) On March 27.
(C) On July 3.
(D) On July 4.

180. What is suggested about Mr. Delaney?
(A) He is the head of a department.
(B) He requested the use of a conference room.
(C) He shares an office with colleagues.
(D) He will work off-site on July 5.

GO ON TO THE NEXT PAGE

WESTFIELD FOOD COOPERATIVE
FARM SHARE PROGRAM

You're Welcome to Join Us!

Westfield Food Cooperative invites you to participate in its community-supported Farm Share program. Members enjoy fresh farm produce during our growing season from April to November. Members receive a farm share once a week. A full-size share is $675, and a half-size share is $350. Half-size shareholders receive half of the full-sized share of produce each week.

Our farm produce is locally-grown without the use of pesticides and herbicides. All producers are Certified Organic.

For more information or to sign up for a share, please visit our Web site, www.westfieldfood.org

Join Farm Share and receive the following benefits:

Lifetime membership to the Westfield Food Cooperative, giving you direct access to local growers and vendors

More than 25 varieties of in-season vegetables, fruits, and herbs, harvested by local producers and delivered fresh to your home by our staff

A selection of pick-your-own citrus fruits, bananas and avocados, and other fruits

Access to our member Web site with updates and a Farm Share newsletter

Discounts on events at the Co-Op for the annual summer music festival. Events cost $15, but members pay $10

WESTFIELD FOOD COOPERATIVE FARM SHARE
REGISTRATION FORM 註冊會員表格

MEMBER INFORMATION

Name: **Kenneth Dolan**

Address: **30048 Arapahoe Drive, Westfield, CO 80032**

Membership plan:
- ● Full share
- ○ Half share

Please provide the names of other individuals in your household. These are the only other individuals who will be permitted to sign for your weekly share:

Lois Dolan, William Dolan

Preferred Delivery Date:
- ○ Thursday
- ○ Friday

CLICK **HERE** TO SUBMIT PAYMENT

* produce
v、① 生產、創作
② 拿出. He produced a bunch of key
from his pocket.
③ 引起. 產生：His arrival produce
a sensation.
他的出現引起轟動

*flyer = leaflet = fly sheet = handbill
= circular
傳單的目標 (目的) 是什麼?

181. What is the purpose of the flyer?
- (D) (A) To invite people to a music festival.
- (B) To promote a new product.
- (C) To recruit summer interns 招募夏季實習
- (D) To advertise a farm program.

182. What is suggested about the workers at Westfield Food Co-op?
- (D) (A) They update the farm's Web site once a week. 一個禮拜更新一次
- (B) They create meals using the farm's (餐點) products. 用農產的產品設計創作食物
- (C) They sell farm products at several local markets. 在幾個當地市集裡賣農場 產品
- (D) They deliver farm produce from April to November. 4月到11月會運送 農產品

183. What is NOT indicated about Westfield Food Co-op?
- (D) (A) It publishes a newsletter.
- (B) It uses natural fertilizers. n.肥料. 使進發展者
- (C) It hosts musical performances. fertilize v.施肥
- (D) It offers cooking classes. ~QI v.使肥沃

184. What is true about Mr. Wentworth's membership?
- (C) (A) He must pick up his produce on Fridays. ~ n.產品. 農產品
- (B) He is the only person who may pick up fruit.
- (C) He is allowed to pick some of his fruit. 可以自己摘水果
- (D) He will be able to plant and grow his own vegetables. 可以自己種植

185. How much should Mr. Wentworth pay for the membership?
- (A) $10.
- (B) $15.
- (C) $350.
- (D) $675.

* recruit
v.微新兵,吸收新成員
恢復健康 (體力)
The rest recruited him.
休息讓他恢復體力
n.新成員.補給品

GO ON TO THE NEXT PAGE.

Questions 186-190 refer to the following advertisements and e-mail.

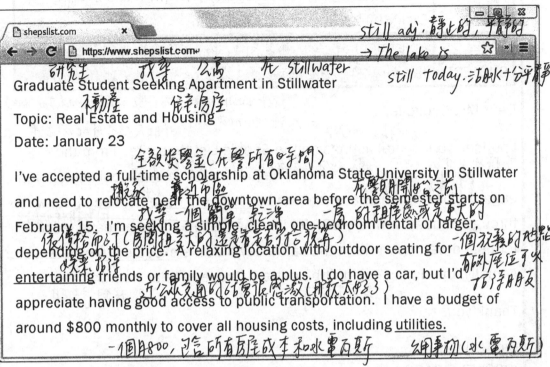

Graduate Student Seeking Apartment in Stillwater

Topic: Real Estate and Housing

Date: January 23

I've accepted a full-time scholarship at Oklahoma State University in Stillwater and need to relocate near the downtown area before the semester starts on February 15. I'm seeking a simple, clean, one-bedroom rental or larger, depending on the price. A relaxing location with outdoor seating for entertaining friends or family would be a plus. I do have a car, but I'd appreciate having good access to public transportation. I have a budget of around $800 monthly to cover all housing costs, including utilities.

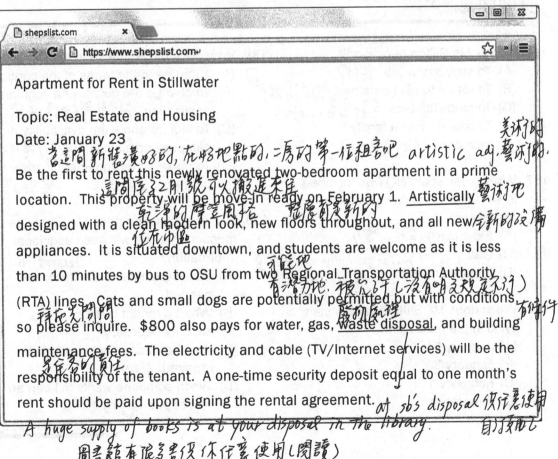

Apartment for Rent in Stillwater

Topic: Real Estate and Housing

Date: January 23

Be the first to rent this newly renovated two-bedroom apartment in a prime location. This property will be move-in ready on February 1. Artistically designed with a clean modern look, new floors throughout, and all new appliances. It is situated downtown, and students are welcome as it is less than 10 minutes by bus to OSU from two Regional Transportation Authority (RTA) lines. Cats and small dogs are potentially permitted but with conditions, so please inquire. $800 also pays for water, gas, waste disposal, and building maintenance fees. The electricity and cable (TV/Internet services) will be the responsibility of the tenant. A one-time security deposit equal to one month's rent should be paid upon signing the rental agreement.

TO	Christine Coolidge <coolidgerental@waymail.com>
FROM	Dick Stilton <r_ctilton@mahal.com>
DATE	Apartment
SUBJECT	January 24

Dear Ms. Coolidge,

I noticed your rental listings on the Shep's List Web site. From the description, it sounds as if it may be just what I've been looking for. I'm eager to look at the apartment, and as luck will have it I'll be in Stillwater through Sunday, January 30. If I like the place and we agree to lease terms, I'd want to move in the same day that it's expected to be available. Actually, the timing couldn't be better! I hope to hear from you soon.

Thank you.

Dick Stilton
(802) 555-0122

186. Why is Mr. Stilton relocating?
(A) To start a new job.
(B) To return to his hometown.
(C) To study full-time.
(D) To take care of a family member.

187. Which cost would NOT be included in Mr. Stilton's rental agreement?
(A) Water.
(B) Electricity.
(C) Gas.
(D) Waste removal.

188. When does Mr. Stilton want to start living in the residence?
(A) January 24.
(B) January 30.
(C) February 1.
(D) February 15.

189. Why does Mr. Stilton send the e-mail?
(A) To agree to the terms of the contract.
(B) To change the details of a scholarship application.
(C) To inquire about the availability of campus services.
(D) To make an arrangement to view the property.

190. For what situation does Ms. Coolidge mention that she will need additional information?
(A) When changes to the décor are needed.
(B) When a tenant is ready to pay a security deposit.
(C) When an apartment needs to be repaired.
(D) When someone wants to keep an indoor pet.

GO ON TO THE NEXT PAGE

American Kitchen Club

Professional equipment at wholesale prices

Hobart AM15-1
Electric High Temp Door-Type Dishwasher

You will never need to buy another dishwasher! Our best-selling model, the AM15-1, is made of easy-to-clean stainless steel and is operated by solid-state controls with digital displays.

Features: The unique door type and hot water/chemical sanitizing design make this professional-grade appliance ideal for busy restaurants of all sizes. Washes up to 56 racks per hour.

Warranty: We include a seven-year warranty on all parts and labor—an assurance to you that our dishwasher will last a long time.

REGULAR PURCHASE PRICE: $10,019.95

UKC MEMBERS: $9,299.95

Handwritten annotations:

wholesale n. 批發
批發: They wholesale the dress at $5 each.
adj. 大批的·大規模的 wholesale slaughter 大規模屠殺
adv. 大批地·大規模地

sanitize 使衛生
The toilet needs to be sanitized. 需要被清潔

熱賣款式 不銹鋼
數位顯示
固態硬碟 (電腦儲存裝置)
特色
化學消毒設計
聯浆
不論大小的生意好的餐廳的最佳選擇 架子

保證、把握、信心 (對自己才能的信心)
→ The teacher has assurance in front of his class.
→ He had the assurance to ask me for money. 厚臉皮 向我要錢

sanitizer n. 清毒劑
sanitary n. 公廁 adj. 公共衛生的
→ He worked hard to improve the sanitary conditions of the slums. 貧民窟

sanitary { napkin / pad / protection / towel } 衛生棉

40

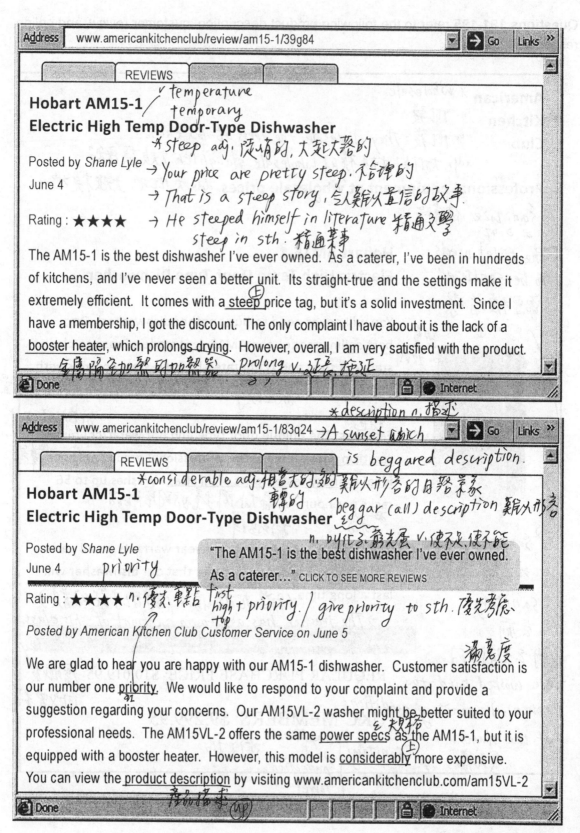

Address www.americankitchenclub/review/am15-1/39g84 Go Links »

REVIEWS

Hobart AM15-1
Electric High Temp Door-Type Dishwasher

Posted by *Shane Lyle*
June 4

Rating : ★★★★

The AM15-1 is the best dishwasher I've ever owned. As a caterer, I've been in hundreds of kitchens, and I've never seen a better unit. Its straight-true and the settings make it extremely efficient. It comes with a steep price tag, but it's a solid investment. Since I have a membership, I got the discount. The only complaint I have about it is the lack of a booster heater, which prolongs drying. However, overall, I am very satisfied with the product.

Done Internet

Address www.americankitchenclub/review/am15-1/83q24 Go Links »

REVIEWS

Hobart AM15-1
Electric High Temp Door-Type Dishwasher

Posted by *Shane Lyle*
June 4

Rating : ★★★★

"The AM15-1 is the best dishwasher I've ever owned. As a caterer..." CLICK TO SEE MORE REVIEWS

Posted by American Kitchen Club Customer Service on June 5

We are glad to hear you are happy with our AM15-1 dishwasher. Customer satisfaction is our number one priority. We would like to respond to your complaint and provide a suggestion regarding your concerns. Our AM15VL-2 washer might be better suited to your professional needs. The AM15VL-2 offers the same power specs as the AM15-1, but it is equipped with a booster heater. However, this model is considerably more expensive. You can view the product description by visiting www.americankitchenclub.com/am15VL-2

Done Internet

GO ON TO THE NEXT PAGE.

191. What is NOT mentioned in the product description as a feature of the AM15-1 dishwasher?

C

(A) It is very efficient. 效率好的
(B) It is suitable for commercial kitchens. 商用廚房適合(做生意的)
(C) It is larger than competitors' dishwashers. 比競爭者的大
(D) It is covered by a warranty. 有保固

192. Why was the AM15VL-2 processor 處理器

D

recommended as being more suitable for Mr. Lyle? 被推薦給Lyle說更適合他呢?
(A) It has a lifetime warranty. 終身保固
(B) It has tube-driven controls.
(C) It has bilingual instructions. 双語指導(手冊) 2 language 2種語言
(D) It has an added feature. 有多的特色(功能)

193. In the online response, the word "regarding" in paragraph 1, line 3, is closest in meaning to

D

(A) in comparison. 比較,對照 (A)
(B) admiring.
(C) looking after. ① 照顧
(D) about. ② 目送

194. What is indicated in the customer review? 評論 檢閱, under review 檢查中

D

(A) American Kitchen Club's customer service is very good.
(B) Users find the AM15-1 difficult to clean. 很難清理
(C) The AM15-1 comes with detailed instructions. 有詳細指示
(D) Mr. Lyle is pleased with his purchase. 很滿意他的購買

195. What is suggested about Mr. Lyle?

D

(A) He purchased some optional parts for the dishwasher. 選擇性零件
(B) He catered a corporate event on June 4. 為公司的活動準備食物
(C) He has never worked in a kitchen before.
(D) He paid $9,299.95 for the dishwasher.

→ there is no comparison 沒法比
can be comparison
→ beyond comparison 無與倫比
→ to make a comparison of sth. 是近對比
   with
→ to draw a comparison with 在~與~之間
   between 相比

CB) admire
v.① 欽佩 欣賞
→ He admires you.
   your poem.
   you for your diplomatic tact.
   外交手腕 ≈ 機智.得體.圓滑
② 誇讚:He admired her new outfit. 誇讚她的新衣服

establishment 建立,確立, 公司,機構

→ The factory is a well-run establishment.
→ (大眾)國家統治集團(體制), 權勢掌控者
The Establishment is trying to hide the truth.

Multimedia
Messaging
Service

AT&T 4:32 PM 82%

Messages **Group MMS** Edit

To: All Artemida Staff **Details**

Attention Everyone: Group Photo This Saturday

Exciting news – The Sagat Dining Guide will be featuring
our restaurant in an article about San Francisco's best
dining establishments!

They have arranged for one of their photographers to
photograph us on Saturday, April 4, at 9:00 a.m., before
preparations for the day begin.

session The court is now in session.
n. 會,集會,會議,會期,請習會,請審班

All employees will be included, so please plan to come
30 minutes earlier than scheduled on Saturday morning
wearing your uniform. The session will take 30 minutes.

We have achieved so much since we opened, and you
should all be very proud of this recognition.

We have achieved so much since we opened, and you
should all be very proud of this recognition.

know
*re|cog|nize v. 認出.認可.承認.表彰

→ The government recognized his outstanding service by
giving him a medal. 政府給他獎章表彰他的傑出服務貢獻
recognizable adj. 可識認出的/承認的
recognizance n.保證金(書)

GO ON TO THE NEXT PAGE.

From:	Jack Ritter <jritter@aperturefocus.com>
To:	Panos Papadopolous <georgio@artemidastaverna.com>
Re:	Saturday Photography Appointment
Date:	April 1

Dear Mr. Papadopolous,

I am writing to confirm your group photography session at 9:00 a.m. on Saturday. As discussed, this photo shoot will take place at your restaurant, and I will photograph your staff along the wall in the main dining hall. You mentioned that you will need to start getting ready for the day at 9:30 a.m., and that should not be a problem. The shoot should be finished by 9:30 a.m.

Please let me know if you have any questions. Otherwise I will see you on Saturday! 我們就周見囉!

Jack Ritter
Aperture Focus, Ltd.

單字補充:

1. It's so great to have the whole gang here _____.
   - ✓ (A) all together 一起、一道
   - (B) altogether adv. 全然.合計

2. Do you have any _____ for a first-time spelunker?
   - ✓ (A) advice n. 建議
   - (B) advise v. 勸告.忠告
   探勘洞穴者

Greek Taverna Delights Potrero Hill

By Noah Pitnik, Staff Writer

Enter Artemida Taverna any day for lunch or dinner, and you'll hear the sound of bouzouki music. "That's the sound of my hometown, Artemida," says Panos Papadopolous, the restaurant's owner.

Opened two years ago, the Taverna has underlined_exceeded expectations. The menu features traditional Greek dishes prepared by chef Voula Markopoulo. She notes, "Our menus feature recipes passed down from one generation to the next." Offering a fresh serving of *spanikopita*, a savory spinach pastry, Markopoulo says, "This is exactly the way it would be served in Panos' home."

On a recent Wednesday afternoon, Yiannis Katsaros, a visitor from Athens, Greece, was dining at the Taverna. "I can't get over the underlined_authenticity of the flavors!" exclaimed Mr. Katsaros. "It's like the chef has taken me back to the old country and I'm dining at my nana's table."

Artemida Taverna is located at 23 DeHaro Street in Potrero Hill, and is open Monday through Saturday from 11:30 a.m. to 10:00 p.m. The interior is painted in the familiar Greek shades of blue and white reminiscent of the ocean, with a rotating gallery of artwork underlined_adorning the walls. The staff is friendly and the delicious food is reasonably priced.

Reservations are not required.

Artemida Taverna, 23 DeHaro Street, Potrero Hill, S.F. Hours: Mon.- Sat. 11:30 a.m. to 10:00 p.m. All major credit cards accepted. (415) 504-3210

GO ON TO THE NEXT PAGE

196. Who most likely posted the notice?

B
(A) Mr. Ritter.
(B) Mr. Papadopolous.
(C) Ms. Markopoulo
(D) Mr. Pitnik.

197. What are employees underline{instructed} to do

A
on April 4?
(A) Arrive earlier than usual. 比平常早到
(B) Work later than usual. 工作比平常晚
(C) Be interviewed for a newspaper article. 為報紙文章面試
(D) Discuss locations for a holiday party. 討論地點

198. What is true about the Artemida

C
Taverna? 每天中午都有開
(A) It is open every day for lunch. 最近經營權
(B) It has recently changed ownership. 改變
(C) It features Greek cuisine. 所有權
(D) It revises the menu seasonally. 每季都會修改菜單

199. What is indicated about the staff?

B
(A) They have been featured in The Sagat Dining Guide more than once.
(B) They will be photographed in the main dining room.
(C) They take turns working the morning shift. 輪流上早班工
(D) They wear brightly colored uniforms. 穿有點上鮮色的制服

200. What does Mr. Katsaros say about the

B
food? 對於份量張夫望
(A) He is disappointed with the portions. 對於口味很驚艷
(B) He is surprised by the flavors.
(C) He saw it featured in a magazine.
(D) He thought it was reasonably priced. 覺得價格合理

to instruct sb. to do sth.
about sth.

＊ instruct v.

1. 指示，命令，吩咐。 He instructed me to deliver it to a customer.

2. 訓練，指導。 My job is to instruct her in English.

3. 通知，告知。 My agent has instructed me that you still own me money.

→ to instruct sb. in 教某人

to instruct sb. how to do sth.

Stop! This is the end of the test. If you finish before time is called, you may go back to Parts 5, 6, and 7 and check your work.

New TOEIC Speaking Test

Question 1: Read a Text Aloud

((◉ 5 ◉)) **Question 1**

Directions: In this part of the test, you will read aloud the text on the screen.
You will have 45 seconds to prepare. Then you will have 45
seconds to read the text aloud.

Looking for a Chinese restaurant that specializes in traditional
Szechuan foods? Then come visit us at Chengdu Garden opening
soon on West Park Boulevard. Our menu features the famous spicy
Szechuan cuisine. All of our unique dishes are prepared from recipes
passed down for generations. The restaurant's opening celebration
will take place on October 10 from 5:00 p.m. to 10:00 p.m. There'll be
food samples and live music. The first 50 guests will be given a free
reusable set of chopsticks with our Chengdu Garden logo. For more
information visit our Web site at www.chengdugarden.com.

PREPARATION TIME
00 : 00 : 45

RESPONSE TIME
00 : 00 : 45

Question 2: Read a Text Aloud

Directions: In this part of the test, you will read aloud the text on the screen. You will have 45 seconds to prepare. Then you will have 45 seconds to read the text aloud.

This morning, another regional hospital announced that it will be closing its mobile health clinic indefinitely. The mobile clinic was designed to improve access to quality health care for people living in the rural areas outside of the city. According to a spokesperson, the hospital ran a mobile health clinic for ten years until forced to shut it down because of budget cutbacks. As budgets for health care are being slashed across the state, authorities are concerned about rural health care, as fewer people will have access to quality services.

[Handwritten annotations: indefinite adj. 無期限的 unknown / unspecified / unlimited / 不確定的 / 行動診所 / 改進,增進健康照顧的品質 / 對於那些住在郊區的人 / 根據發言人 / 營運超過10年了 / 直到被迫關閉 / 預算 減少 由於 / slash 苦向 開心 urban / 農村的 / 田園的 / 只有比較少的人能夠接觸 / 到有品質的服務 / 砍、撑 減少、批評 / Some critics slashed his new book.]

PREPARATION TIME
00 : 00 : 45

RESPONSE TIME
00 : 00 : 45

GO ON TO THE NEXT PAGE.

Question 3: Describe a Picture

Question 3

Directions: In this part of the test, you will describe the picture on your screen in as much detail as you can. You will have 30 seconds to prepare your response. Then you will have 45 seconds to speak about the picture.

PREPARATION TIME
00 : 00 : 30

RESPONSE TIME
00 : 00 : 45

答題範例

🎧 6 ▶ **Question 3**

I see a number of people on the street. *苦不一些*

This appears to be a film shoot on location. *拍攝外景的*

There is some filming equipment on the sidewalk. *= pavement = footpath* *by way 偏僻小路*

strategic 戰略的, 關鍵的 = strategical

Traffic cones are placed strategically around the scene.

Two men dressed in black appear to be actors. *adj. 雜亂的, 隨意的*

A car with a siren on the roof is parked haphazardly at the curb. *汽迪. 警報器* *① n. 路邊*

公告牌. 標語 *② v控制 通膨 to curb inflation*

There are numbered placards on the sidewalk.

Wires and cables run through the street.

There are a number of unidentified objects strewn about. *Strew strewed strewh*

電線. 電話線. 電纜 *object n. 物體 object v. 反對 目標* *撒. 播. 使散落*

Several men are standing near or attending to the camera.

Several other people are standing nearby in conversation. *注意. 致力於 關心. 護理*

The director appears to be approaching one of the actors.

停播. 散布

There is a very large, dark object in the upper-right of the picture.

It's being used to diffuse ambient light. *周遭的*

In the left foreground is a fire escape.

Also in the foreground, a sign offering spa services and massage.

A truck can be seen in the far upper-right corner of the frame.

Someone has spray painted lines around a box in the roadway.

噴霧 *軌道*

GO ON TO THE NEXT PAGE ➡

Questions 4-6: Respond to Questions

答題範例

《 6 》 Question 4

What's the weather like this time of year?

每年這個時候的天氣大概是怎麼樣的?

Answer

> It's summertime. 夏季
>
> So, it's going to be very hot.
>
> Also, be prepared for rain. 為下雨做好準備 (可能會下雨)

《 6 》 Question 5

What type of clothing is appropriate for sightseeing?

要觀光的話穿什麼衣服合適?

Answer

> 輕鬆的. 休閒的 衣服 是最好的
> Light and casual clothing is best.
>
> Most people dress for comfort. 大部分都穿著舒適服裝
>
> A good pair of walking sandals would be helpful.
> 又 涼鞋. 拖鞋

GO ON TO THE NEXT PAGE.

Questions 4-6: Respond to Questions

 **Question 6**

If I need to buy clothing during my visit, where should I go, and why?

Answer

有很多地方可以買便宜的衣服
There are many places to buy cheap clothing here.

夜市是買衣服很方便的地方
The night market is a convenient place to shop for clothing.

你也可以去好多家商場中的其中一間
You could also go to one of the many malls in the city.

h. 衣服
If you have time, there's a special garment district near the

train station. a block of 大宗. 大塊. He holds a block of

一大塊區工或除了衣服沒有別的   share.
It's a whole city block of nothing but clothing.   擁有大宗股票

It's almost overwhelming.

壓倒的. 勢不可擋的. 難以忍受的

A lot of people like to shop at Sogo.

所有頂級品牌都有賣
It's a department store that sells all the top brands.

You might want to check it out. 可以去看看

Questions 7-9: Respond to Questions Using Information Provided

《 5 》 **Question 7**

Directions: In this part of the test, you will answer three questions based on the information provided. You will have 30 seconds to read the information before the questions begin. For each question, begin responding immediately after you hear a beep. No additional preparation time is provided. You will have 15 seconds to respond to Questions 7 and 8 and 30 seconds to respond to Question 9.

後活節　周日　早午餐

EASTER SUNDAY BRUNCH

商業貿易

Please join Taiwanease.com, The Canadian Chamber of Commerce and the Swiss Association of Taiwan for our annual Easter brunch at The Tavern. The last few years have been great affairs. The kids always have a wonderful time, and the parents do too!

事情,件 It's my affair,是我的事　　　小酒館

As in past years, the event starts at 1:00 PM and goes to 4:00 PM. There will be an Easter egg hunt in the nearby park at 2:00——this is something that the kids love.

The prices are: $550 for adults, $300 for kids over 115 cm, and free for those under!

Full brunch buffet with all your favorites, including carved Easter ham with soft drinks and unlimited coffee and tea from 1:00 to 3:00.　Carve v.雕;切　軟性飲料

For adults, all draught beers are buy one, get one free.

生啤酒　　買一送一

Program:
1:00 PM to 3:00 PM – Buffet is open
2:00 PM – All kids gather and go to the park for the Easter Egg Hunt　在公園裡集合,找蛋
3:00 PM – Egg painting for the kids, supervised by adults 小朋友塗姿油蛋. 大人看看。

The Tavern is located at 415 Xinyi Road, Section 4

Hi, I'm interested in the Easter Brunch. Would you mind if I asked a few questions?

PREPARATION TIME
00 : 00 : 30

Question 7 Q	uestion 8	Question 9
RESPONSE TIME	**RESPONSE TIME**	**RESPONSE TIME**
00 : 00 : 15	00 : 00 : 15	00 : 00 : 30

GO ON TO THE NEXT PAGE. ➡

Questions 7-9: Respond to Questions Using Information Provided

答題範例

🎧 6 🎧 **Question 7**

When does the event take place? 這個活動在哪裡舉行

Answer

> 發生
> The brunch takes place on Easter Sunday.
>
> It starts at 1:00 PM. 一點鐘開始
>
> It usually ends around 4:00 PM. 通常四點結束

🎧 6 🎧 **Question 8**

Who can attend? 誰可以參加？

Answer

> Anybody! 任何人都可以參加
> We have activities for the kids. 有給小孩子的活動
> And parents usually enjoy themselves as well.
>
> 通常大人也和孩子們一樣享受

Questions 7-9: Respond to Questions Using Information Provided

🎧 6 **Question 9**

What is included in the price?

價格包含了什麼項目?

Answer

(用以繼續原來的話題 or 引入新的話題) 這個喉舌

Well, first of all, there's the food. 首先,有食物

It's all you can eat. 是吃到飽的

The buffet includes Easter ham with soft drinks and

unlimited coffee and tea. 不限量的咖啡和茶

There will be an Easter egg hunt in the nearby park at 附近的公園

2:00. ✳ supervise v.

This is something that the kids love. supervisor n. 管理人 監督人

Adult supervision will be provided. 管理, 監督 supervisal 監督的

supervisory 管理員的 的 監督人的

Finally, there is a drink special. 有特殊飲品 →

All draught beers are buy one get, one free.

Hope to see you there!

GO ON TO THE NEXT PAGE.➜

Question 10: Propose a Solution

Directions: In this part of the test, you will be presented with a problem and asked to propose a solution. You will have 30 seconds to prepare. Then you will have 60 seconds to speak. In your response, be sure to show that you recognize the problem, and propose a way of dealing with the problem.

In your response, be sure to
- show that you recognize the caller's problem, and
- propose a way of dealing with the problem.

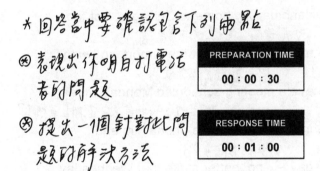

★ 回答當中要確認包含下列兩點
㊟ 表現出你明白打電話者的問題

PREPARATION TIME

00 : 00 : 30

㊟ 提出一個針對此問題的解決方法

RESPONSE TIME

00 : 01 : 00

Question 10: Propose a Solution

答題範例

6 ▶ Question 10

Voice Message

Hi Kristen, this is Benjamin. I need to stay in Seattle a
我需要多留在西雅圖幾天

要把這個案子完成

你可以取消我的班機

couple extra days to finalize this deal. Could you please

然後幫我訂周五晚上的飛機喔

cancel my flight tonight and book me on a Friday night flight

從西雅圖到奧州

from Seattle to Oklahoma City? Then, I'll need a Sunday

evening flight from Oklahoma City home to Chicago. Not too

不要訂太晚的   我太會在機場和我見面

late please. I'll have my wife meet me at the airport, so I won't

不需要載我   周一有預訂的會議

need a ride. Also, I have a meeting scheduled Monday with

打給他重新安排到週四

Mr. Morgan from Glenn & Glenn. Please phone him and

喔不.同三的3.

reschedule until Tuesday——no, better make that Wednesday,

以免我被延誤了   現在呢.不要轉傳任何

in case I get delayed in Oklahoma City. For now, don't forward

訊息給我,除非很緊急   迫切的,強迫的,緊急的.

any messages to me unless they're <u>urgent</u>. I'll be in

=pressing =compelling = imperative

negotiations all day tomorrow and Friday. If you need to reach 急迫

如果你要找我.打給我留言即可

me, call my cell phone and leave a message. Thanks Kristen.

I'll see you Monday morning.

GO ON TO THE NEXT PAGE.

Question 10: Propose a Solution

答題範例

Hi Benjamin, I got your message.

Sorry to hear that you're stuck in Seattle. 報歉(很遺憾)聽到你

卡在西雅圖的消息

被耽擱

I've got things under control in the office.
一切都在我掌握之中

I got in touch with the airline this morning. 今早和航空公司聯繫

I've got you booked on the 9:30 p.m. flight out of Seattle.

You'll be in Oklahoma City before midnight. 午夜前會到

The Sunday evening flight is a bit tricky. 狡滑的, 微妙的
期廋棹的

The only evening flight from Oklahoma City leaves at 5:30 p.m.

Is that late enough for you? 對你來說夠晚嗎?

取消這底/   /limousine
I went ahead and canceled your limo on Friday.

They told me there is a 50% late cancellation fee. 有5%延遲取消

Did you know about that? 你知道這件事嗎   費用

Meanwhile, I got in touch with Mr. Morgan. 我聯络上了 Mr. Morgan.

He can't do Wednesday.

So, I scheduled a meeting for Thursday afternoon. 我安排了周四
下午的會議

There really hasn't been anything urgent lately.

If there is, I'll let you know. 如果有, 我會讓你知道

Call me when you have a minute. 有空時打给我吧!

Question 11: Express an Opinion

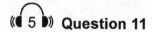 **Question 11**

Directions: In this part of the test, you will give your opinion about a specific topic. Be sure to say as much as you can in the time allowed. You will have 15 seconds to prepare. Then you will have 60 seconds to speak.

禁止　　同性婚姻　　一些国家开始的程序　同性的面的禁令

Some countries are lifting the ban on same-sex marriage. Do you support

removing

the idea or oppose it? Give reasons to support your answer.

你支持或是反对呢? 意出支持你答案的理由.

PREPARATION TIME
00 : 00 : 15

RESPONSE TIME
00 : 01 : 00

GO ON TO THE NEXT PAGE

Question 11: Express an Opinion

答題範例

《6》 Question 11

我完全支持這個想法
I fully support the idea.

如果二個男人/女人都要結婚這完全不關別人的事
It is no one else's business if two men or two women want to get married.

Two people who love each other should be allowed to publicly celebrate their commitment.
2個相愛的人應被允許公開慶祝他們的承諾

同性情侶應得到一樣的福利如同異性情侶
Same sex couples deserve to receive the same benefits of marriage as opposite sex couples.

有些人可能會說如果他們結婚會威脅到傳統婚姻的價值
Some people say that allowing them to marry threatens the value of "traditional marriage."

However, I believe there is no such thing as traditional marriage.
然而,我相信沒有所謂"傳統婚姻"這件事

There are many examples of family arrangements based on polygamy and communal
共同的,共有的
child-rearing. 養小孩

在現今社會中還是有很多地方是這樣的 一夫多妻、一妻多夫
This is still practiced in many parts of current society.

In that sense, monogamy can be considered "unnatural" in evolutionary terms.
一夫一妻制   不自然的   發展的,進化的,漸進的

Gay marriage is protected by the Constitution. 同性婚姻是被憲法保護的

The freedom of personal choice is protected by the Due Process Clause.

Therefore, banning gay marriage is unconstitutional. 禁止同性婚姻是違反憲法的

污辱,給…帶來恥辱
Denying same-sex couples the right to marry stigmatizes gay and lesbian families.

It implies that it is acceptable to discriminate against them.

It assigns them to second-class status. 有差別的對待;區別;區分

可以帶來財政上的好處
Finally, gay marriages can bring financial gain to state and local governments. 更高的收入稅

Revenue from gay marriage comes from marriage licenses and higher income taxes.

What's more, gay marriage will make it easier for same-sex couples to adopt children.

New TOEIC Writing Test

Questions 1-5: Write a Sentence Based on a Picture

Question 1

Directions: Write ONE sentence based on the picture using the TWO words or phrases under it. You may change the forms of the words and you may use them in any order.

rider / helmet

1. All of the riders are wearing helmets.
2. All bicycle riders should wear helmets.
3. The people riding the bicycles are wearing helmets.

Questions 1-5: Write a Sentence Based on a Picture

Question 2

Directions: Write ONE sentence based on the picture using the TWO words or phrases under it. You may change the forms of the words and you may use them in any order.

camp / scout

camp
n. 營地；帳篷；陣營
v. 紮營，露營

scout
n. 童子軍
v. 偵察；搜索；不信
→ They were chosen to scout the trail.
→ Most scientists scouted the new theory.
不信這個新的理論

1. The boy scouts are camping.

2. The scouts have set up a camp.

(b) 好人：He's a good scout.

3. The scouts are in camp.

GO ON TO THE NEXT PAGE.

Questions 1-5: Write a Sentence Based on a Picture

Question 3

Directions: Write ONE sentence based on the picture using the TWO words or phrases under it. You may change the forms of the words and you may use them in any order.

dog / stroller

Stroller 閒逛的人, 摺疊式嬰兒車

stroll v. 散步 : I used to stroll along the beach on Sundays.

　　　 n. ✓ : He took a stroll after supper.

1. The dog is in the stroller.

2. A person is pushing a stroller that contains a dog.

3. The dog is sitting in the stroller.

Questions 1-5: Write a Sentence Based on a Picture

Question 4

Directions: Write ONE sentence based on the picture using the TWO words or phrases under it. You may change the forms of the words and you may use them in any order.

passenger / pregnant

* pregnant
adj. ① 懷孕的 ② 富有的 → He is a man pregnant with ideas.
　　③ 意義深長的 → His words were followed by a pregnant pause.
　　→ a pregnant decision 有結論的決定

1. The female passenger is pregnant.
2. One of the passengers is pregnant.
3. The pregnat passenger is sitting in the aisle seat.
　　　　　　　　　　　　　　(走道)

GO ON TO THE NEXT PAGE.

Questions 1-5: Write a Sentence Based on a Picture

Question 5

Directions: Write ONE sentence based on the picture using the TWO words or phrases under it. You may change the forms of the words and you may use them in any order.

stairs / students

1. Some students are climbing the stairs.
2. The students are on the stairs.
3. All of the students are going up the stairs.

go up ①.上去 ②被建造起来 = New factories are going up everywhere.

③焚毁 = The whole building went up in flames.

Questions 6-7: Respond to a written request

Question 6

Directions: Read the e-mail below.

From: Justine Frankl, Director of Personnel 偵、員工	
To: David Reedus, CEO *chief executive officer* 總裁、執行長	
Re: Budget meeting	*concern* n. 關心的事、重要的事 That's no concern of mine.
Sent: April 26 v. 涉及到	擔心 關懷 He expressed his concern.

關係到：The news concerns your brother.
影響到
look over 係細檢查 使擔心：His poor health concerned his parents.

David,

Looking over the budget, I have some concerns. First, while the
overall spending for the past three-month period was within our
budget, an alarming decrease in the amount spent on recruitment is
cause for concern. With peak production starting in June, we need
to be fully staffed. Therefore, I would like to schedule a meeting to
discuss our workforce outlook for the rest of the year.

① 觀點 ② 看法 ③ 展望 ④ 前景 The economic outlook is bright.

The proposed meeting would take place tomorrow at 9:30 a.m. in

Conference Room B. Please let me know if you have a scheduling

conflict.

⑤ 景色、風光：The room has a pleasant outlook.
⑥ 注視、瞭望：She is always on the outlook for a better opportunity.

Thanks,

Justine

比…好看
His horse outlooked all the others in the race.

While conj. ①當…時 ②然而 ③雖然、儘管 ④只要

Directions: Write back to Ms. Frankl as Mr. Reedus. Give ONE reason
why you cannot attend the meeting, and address her
concerns about the budget. 提出、向~致詞

GO ON TO THE NEXT PAGE.

答題範例

Question 6

Justine,

不幸的是. *我會參加會議而且我整個周五會參加比銷售會議*

Unfortunately, I will not be able to attend a meeting tomorrow as I will be

attending a sales conference in Chicago through Friday, and will not be

back at headquarters until next Monday.   clarify sewage   污水
總部.局.總公司   澄清.闡明.淨化   /sjuɪdʒ/ 汙穢物

However, I would like to clarify the recruitment situation and explain the

dramatic expense decrease. As of the end of February, we had received

approximately 300% of our estimated applications for open positions. In
換言之   不需要再拓展更多的可能的員工
other words, we didn't need to recruit any more potential employees.

Thus, our expenses were significantly lower. I hope this clears things up.

Sincerely,   * dramatic   adv: 意味深長地.顯著地   澄清
David   戲劇般的   * significant   解釋
              充滿激情的   adj. ① 有意義的   清理
              誇張的   ② 表示…的 = Smiles are significant   放晴
              引人注目的   ③ 重大的   of pleasure.

* position
位置. 職位. 情勢. 情況
地位: He has a high position in society.
立場: What's your position on this problem?
       針對這個問題你的立場是什麼?

Questions 6-7: Respond to a written request

Question 7

Directions: Read the e-mail below.

From: Thad Sayer
To: Greg Espinoza
Date: Thursday, July 23
Subject: Phone issues

Greg,

I'm writing to discuss an issue related to my recent move to room 7054. I've taken over Daisy Cooper's old office and phone number, as she has taken an extended leave from work. Apparently, customers were not informed about this, and consequently, I have received, on average, over thirty calls a day from her customer accounts. It appears as though the employee directory has not yet been changed to let them know that: (A) She is not here; and (B) Stan Feldspar is handling her accounts in the meantime. To have to take so many calls that are not intended for me is so time-consuming and distracting. Would it be possible to change the extension number or connect my old extension number 5-7025, to room 7054? I would greatly appreciate your help.

Thank you very much.

Thad Sayer

Directions: Reply as Greg Espinoza and acknowledge but decline Thad Sayer's request. Give ONE reason and ONE possible solution.

GO ON TO THE NEXT PAGE.

Questions 6-7: Respond to a written request

答題範例

Question 7

Thad,

以 發行, 配給, 出版

bring sth. to one's attention

n. 問題, 事件, 爭論, 爭議, 子女 → to inform one of sth.

I understand your issue and I appreciate you bringing it to my attention.

distract 分心   interrupt 打擾

I'm sure the distractions and interruptions must be frustrating, not to

反向地, 相反地

mention, counter-productive. Unfortunately, I am not able to

符合, 滿足   產生不良後果的

accommodate you at this time, as our phone system is due to be

love 'h/l 大修, 拆開檢修

completely overhauled next month, which means, a week from

因此   我不再有權利去改變現在的系統

tomorrow. Therefore, I'm no longer authorized to make changes to

好消息是你會被分派一個新的, 永久的

the existing system. The good news is you will be assigned a new,

永久的   分機

permanent extension that will follow you wherever you work in the

= lasting = durable = long-lasting ⟷ impermanent, momentary

company. This should make your life a lot easier. In the meantime,

我也更新了公司的電話簿   Temporary

I've updated the company directory, and I've asked Stan Feldspar to

聯繫 Daisy 的客戶 讓他們知道這個改變

contact all of Daisy's clients and let them know about the change.

Thanks for your patience,

Greg

Questions 8: Write an opinion essay

Question 8

Directions: Read the question below. You have 30 minutes to plan, write, and revise your essay. Typically, an effective response will contain a minimum of 300 words.

運輸、送、交通費

Choose one of the following transportation vehicles and explain why

you think it has changed people's lives.

We paid out transportation to Taipei.

- Automobiles 對人類生活的影響
- Bicycles 就會提到該交通工具
- Airplanes 的優缺點

我們付了到台比的交通费

★車: ⓑ ease of transportation

fast commute from one place to another

ⓧ
increase in pollution

decrease in practices such as walking and cycling

expensive to buy, expensive to maintain

★腳踏車 ⓑ

great for exercise

low cost

doesn't pollute the environment

faster than walking and no slower than a car in cities

壞
difficult to move large or multiple items.

not quick over long distances

GO ON TO THE NEXT PAGE.

Questions 8: Write an opinion essay

Question 8

There have been many vehicles since the invention of the wheel that changed the world in many ways, but airplanes have made the greatest impact on the lives of all human beings, be it directly or indirectly. The effect can be felt in almost all types of industry, including travel and tourism, satellite and communication, and business and commerce. Airplanes are now the preferred solution for long-distance travel and thousands of flights are operated in airports around the world every day.

In addition, airplanes changed warfare completely and absolutely, which changed the course of history, many times over. A lot of strategic bombing has been replaced nowadays with cruise missile technology, but tactical bombing still seems to be the norm. There are also drones (remotely piloted unmanned aerial vehicles) which have brought about their own well-known changes to warfare. The impact of war cannot be overstated.

Commercially, jet aircraft revolutionized travel. It killed the ocean liners (ships designed to expeditiously move passengers from a port of origin to a different destination—as opposed to cruise ships, which typically operate to move leisure travelers through a loop back to the point of origin). It makes a trip to the other side of the world (and back) a realistic vacation within the reach of many ordinary people, instead of something reserved for the ultrawealthy with yachts and no jobs. It makes the travel part of emigration across oceans a short flight, instead of a month's long voyage on a ship. It has opened up worldwide markets for perishable goods (the flowers in my supermarket here in the U.S. may have been in Amsterdam the day before, and in the Congo the day before that—try that with the fastest ocean liner).

Light (general aviation) aircraft give so much benefit to their local communities. They include air ambulance helicopters and corporate aircraft that move executives swiftly and efficiently as they manage regional business concerns. In the oil industry, light aircraft efficiently patrol pipelines to watch for leaks, monitor construction activity that could compromise underground pipelines, and bring in parts for critical repairs. They can also provide aerial surveillance of crops and ranch herds in agribusiness. Air travel is at the core of all these benefits.

Another aspect affected by airplanes is pollution, particularly air pollution. Airplanes emit toxic gases while flying and especially during landing and takeoff. These gases demolish the ozone layer, leading to global warming. However, ground access vehicles such as passenger cars and buses just entering and leaving the airport often exceed airplanes as the dominant sources of air pollution at airports.

It is clear that airplanes have changed the world, but it has come at a certain cost.